Science fiction magazine

We're supporting

and we thank Cymera for supporting us.

ISSN 2059-2590

ISBN 978-1-9993331-4-0

Shoreline of Infinity is available in digital and print editions.
Submissions of fiction, art, reviews, poetry, non-fiction are welcomed: visit
the website to find out how to submit.

www.shorelineofinfinity.com

Publisher

Shoreline of Infinity Publications / The New Curiosity Shop
Edinburgh
Scotland

260519

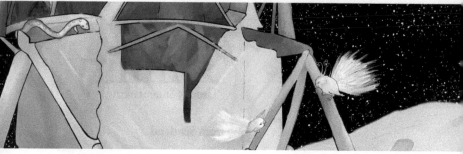

Contents

Cover: Becca McCall

Shoreline of Infinity
Science Fiction Magazine
Editorial Team

Co-founder, Editor-in-Chief & Editor:
Noel Chidwick

Co-founder, Art Director:
Mark Toner

Deputy Editor & Poetry Editor:
Russell Jones

Reviews Editor:
Samantha Dolan

Assistant Editors:
Monica Burns, Pippa Goldschmidt

Copy editors:
Andrew J Wilson, Iain Maloney,
Russell Jones, Monica Burns, Pippa
Goldschmidt

Manifold thanks to: Richard Ridgwell

First Contact

www.shorelineofinfinity.com

contact@shorelineofInfinity.com

Twitter: @shoreinf

and on Facebook

Pull Up a Log

When Mark Toner and I started *Shoreline of Infinity Science Fiction Magazine* we wondered where it would take us. Apparently, it takes us to Holyrood. This is the home of the Scottish Parliament where we have an exhibition of the brilliant artwork we've published over the last few years. We're here for a few days, and it's a chance to show off Shoreline of Infinity to the great and the good in Government. We're also talking up science fiction and its value in this maddening world, and it has giving us the opportunity to wheel out our favourite (dated, but pertinent) Arthur C. Clarke quote:

"Politicians should read science fiction, not westerns and detective stories."

Shoreline of Infinity has brought us to Cymera – Scotland's first science fiction, fantasy and horror book festival. This too has been a real journey to arrive at the point where Edinburgh welcomes writers and readers to celebrate the written word of the fantastical. All credit to the director, Ann Landmann, who has put her heart, soul and more besides into making Cymera happen. Shoreline of Infinity are proud to be a part of helping to bring Cymera to life.

And one of our other favourite destinations is where we can announce the winners of the Cymera/Shoreline of Infinity short story competition for unpublished Scottish based writers. Congratulations go to Cleo Luna and Beth Nuttall: you'll find their terrific tales further along in these pages.

Right – where next? We have ideas... We hope you, dear reader, continue on this journey with us.

—*Noel Chidwick, Editor-in-Chief*
Shoreline of Infinity
June 2019

Secret Ingredients

Callum McSorley

I'm a line cook. This is how I became a spy:
I come from a binary solar system. We don't have what other beings might call day and night. Nor do we measure days like they measure days, or years like they measure years. I can't tell you how old I am, not in a way that would satisfy you. All I can say is, the first time I saw the dark – the real, deep dark – was the first time I left home. I looked out at the obsidian void from the window of the ship, and knew I was gone and never going back. Goodbye, Mama. Goodbye, Papa.

The job was waiting for me: Barkbere's Bistro. The restaurant was in an old ship which had landed by the bay, disgorging the first inhabitants of Nilvur. These were Barkbere's ancestors. I don't know how long ago this was, but it was Barkbere senior who advertised the job and Barkbere junior who was running the place when I arrived.

He was a well-dressed crustacean who lived in his office, the former captain's quarters. When we finally met, he looked at me as if he wanted to run his feelers over my skin. "A humie," he said. His throat clicked as he spoke. "I've never hired a humie before. Dad must have had his reasons."

I started to expound on my resumé, but he held up a claw for silence. I dry swallowed my words, my memorised and polished speech on craft, passion and teamwork going down like a half-chewed hunk of meat.

"A trial," he said, nodding. His eyelids flickered. With that, I was sent to the kitchen. I passed through the dining room, still carrying my backpack with all my worldly belongings inside – a second suit and a set of knives. Empty for now, it was a great, saucer-shaped room lit by glowing insects stuffed into jars that hung from the ceiling. There were seats and tables shaped to accommodate all kinds of customers. Beings travelled far to eat at Barkbere's, even from offworld.

The restaurant might have been empty, but the kitchen was already clanking and churning and howling away. I could hear it before I pushed through the swing doors. When I did, nobody looked up, nobody stopped working, nobody noticed. The closest I got to a greeting was a huge hammerhead screeching "Back!" at me as he passed carrying a tank of slithering eels, which flickered and sparked their annoyance at being sloshed around. They would be more annoyed later when they were tipped, still alive, into the fryolator.

"Excuse me," I shouted, "where is the chef?"

"Chef's right here," a voice said behind me. Chef was a vigintipede. His whites looked like bandages wrapped around his insect body. A missing limb in his top half was conspicuous. There were many rumours about how Chef came to lose that arm, from bar fights to kitchen accidents, but nobody knew the truth, probably because nobody asked him. Chef had the eyes of a murderer, but his voice, when he wasn't calling out orders, was soft and malicious, like a pillow pressed over your face. You didn't ask Chef to repeat an order, and you didn't ask Chef about his missing arm.

"I'm Grith," I said, "I'm here for the line cook job."

"Are you?"

"Yes."

"No."

"Sorry?"

"The pot wash is over here." Three arms pointed the way.

That's how I started out at Barkbere's: in the pot wash. Barkbere was right, it was a trial. Scrubbing out burnt pots with sand and steel wool is hard work, never mind scraping the dried gunk off plates stacked up way over your head. In those early days, I didn't sleep. The only food I ate was the 'family meal' – trays of whatever was going off were roasted in the pressure oven, and left out to congeal and go cold for whoever was hungry enough to eat it.

There were staff quarters in the bistro – former dorms of the colonists – in the outer carousel of the ship. I spent most of my little free time there. One night I heard a knock at the door and opened it to find Scully the broilerman outside. "You like fishing?" he asked.

"I've never tried," I said.

It was twilight, the single sun casting an orange and pink glow over everything. "Best to fish when it gets dark," Scully said. We tramped out the delivery entrance and down towards the beach. The sand was silver and smooth, and felt nearly indistinguishable from the seawater when I ran my fingers through it.

Across the bay, I could see winking lights among the trees that grew brighter as the sunlight died. "Is that the Hideaway?" I asked.

Scully answered with a single word: "Bastards."

The Hideaway was as famous as Barkbere's, maybe more so. It attracted the same intergalactic clientele, and had a similar menu of classic Nilvurian dishes tuned up to fine-dining standard. Both fished out of the same bay, staring each other out from opposite banks across the calm quicksilver expanse of the sea. The Hideaway was a common topic of conversation in the Barkbere kitchen during prep time. The cooks wished infestations on them and hatched plans to drive them out of business, or at least embarrass them. *They think they're better than us*, was the general mentality.

"Is there a boat?" I asked.

Scully, an octosapian from Orion's orbit, laughed, stripped off his whites, and waded into the water until he was up to his waist. I undressed and followed him in. The water was cold, but that wasn't what gave me discomfort. It was the prickling sensation that worried me. It felt like the burnished, grey water was eating me.

"Watch," Scully said, as the sun dropped behind the trees and the sky went fully dark. I still wasn't used to that. You can see the stars when it's dark. You look up and you see outer space. It made me dizzy.

The sea switched on, the metal sheen now glowing with ethereal turquoise light. "Bioluminescence – that's why we wait till dark to catch the fish," Scully said. My eyes were getting used to the sudden, dazzling glow of the sea, and I began to make out the shapes moving under the surface, the stripes of eerie, glowing light on the sides of the lake creatures as they darted in the water.

"How do we catch them?" I asked.

"Like so," Scully said. A tentacle lashed out into the water, causing sluggish waves that turned into a simmering churn as the tentacle wrapped itself around a flashing fish and hoisted it out. He tossed it onto a bedsheet that he'd spread out on the beach. The lights on the fish went out.

I had a shot. I waited for the shining blue stripes to stray close, and then dove in with both hands, the water splashing in my eyes and stinging. Spluttering and soaking, I came up empty. Scully laughed and I tried again. And I missed and missed and thrashed around in the water.

"You go for a swim," Scully said, "I'll tend to business." It was fun. I got my fingers around something that slipped out as if I'd clapped my hands on a stick of butter. That was the closest I got to a catch, meanwhile Scully had piled up a slithering, tangling mass of scaled bodies with fins and pincers and dead, jelly eyes. He pulled up three or four fish at a time, his tentacles moving independently of each other.

When we had enough, I helped him haul the catch back to the kitchen. My skin and hair were covered in a grey crust that peeled off in the shower. I felt grit in my teeth for days afterwards.

There were two defining moments for me that first season. The first was the stock pot incident. Back home, I could lift a big pot by myself, but on Nilvur, the gravity is stronger, a factor I forgot to account for, and sent a whole pot of crab stock crashing over the floor in a fragrant, orange wave. Scully screamed at me. June the fryer screamed at me. Krik, the hammerhead and sauce expert, swung a cleaver at my head. Chef just stared, and that was the worst. I swept the stock into the drains that ran along the foot of each station, and kept my head down for several shifts. Any time an order came through for lake-tarantula bisque, shame turned my stomach.

The second came not longer after. Having four tentacles as arms made Scully an ideal broilerman. He worked on a huge range with twelve burners, his left tentacles whipping out to shake pans and stir pots while his right ones dove into the low-boy fridges or swept the speed shelves above his head for seasonings. I was bringing him a clean pan when a jumping jack, true to its name, leapt from the roasting pan and fell between the burning rings. A tentacle went after it in a reflex motion, and Scully howled as the searing heat burned his suckers. I put the clean pan down at the station and reached in between the green flames of the gas burners, grabbing hold of the jumping jack with my bare hand. Then I put it back into the pan and strolled back to the pot wash without a word, feeling the eyes – including both of Krik's – on my back. Beings where I come from – with two suns and no night-time and no winter season – are pretty much heat-proof. The pain was minimal, but I didn't tell them that.

Not long after, I was bumped up to prep cook, and then, by the start of next season, I was a line cook, making cold starters. However, it was decided that this was a waste of my individual attributes, and I became Scully's assistant at the broiler station. Barkbere was so impressed by his first humie that he hired another to replace me in the pot wash. This one was as white as I am black, with a shock of orange hair on his head, and spots all over his face and arms. He spoke the local language with an odd accent, but often reverted to whatever it was his kind spoke whenever he was under pressure. It came out in a jagged, nasal burr that sounded something like, "Yefuk'nbas'trtyeabsylootprikyefuk'nmoovyererce…" All in all, he was a disagreeable man, but he'd been working on a nearby planet and was available at short notice.

Around this time, a media war was brewing between us and them across the bay. We were both courting tables of critics – vultures who picked and pecked at their dishes with painted beaks, and left piles of clay droppings on the floor behind them. Barkbere took to storming into the kitchen and berating us when there were fewer and fewer guests – important guests, that is, guests who mattered – to schmooze with front of house.

"We're losing," Barkbere said, the red of his carapace turning redder. "Why are we losing?"

"Scrafulax," Chef said, in his deathly quiet voice, placid as the reservoir that lures you in on a hot day only to tangle you up in the weeds hidden beneath and drown you.

Chef was right. Scrafulax was the hot thing, *the* dish you needed to be serving. Scrafulax was a mollusc found in the deep oceans of Nilvur, dredged by squids – although Scully claimed an octosapian like himself could do it too. It looked unassuming enough, a gooey, kidney-shaped white blob covered with a see-through silky membrane inside a craggy, rock-like shell. The problem was that they were poisonous. Deadly poisonous, with a kill-rate of something like one in four. And yet, the Hideaway had them on the menu. They must have found a way to make scrafulax safe. It was destroying us. The vultures stopped coming.

Barkbere took me into his office. Chef was there too. They looked like they were going to snuff me. Barkbere clicked his pincers. His feelers were trained on me. "You've been doing a great job here, Grith," he said.

"Thank you, sir."

"How are you enjoying working on the line?"

"I love it, sir, the opportunity to – "

Chef held up a couple of hands to shut me up.

"Good, that's good," Barkbere said, clacking away, "but I have another job for you. Over at the Hideaway."

"What?"

Chef held up his hands again.

"They've heard about your … special talent…" – again I felt like his feelers wanted to explore my skin – "…and want to poach you from me. We're going to let them."

There was plenty about this plan that I didn't like. It had been hard enough to prove myself to the hardcore of the Barkbere cooks, and now I'd be back to the start with a whole new crew of tyrannical maniacs who thought little of humies and even less of former Barkbere employees. Also, I wasn't lying when I told the old lobster that I was enjoying my work on the line. Sure, I had been bullied and intimidated: I spent every morning cleaning and dehorning saltwater cacti that squirted a rank-smelling oil over you if sliced wrong. Yes, I was cut and bruised and worked half to death, and the hours were still long and the shifts still manic, but I finally felt at home. I was having fun. Masochistic fun, of course, but fun all the same. And when the team were on, we were really *on*. It was like a dance, the way we moved, the way we coordinated. Me and Scully were two parts of the same cook. The food we turned out was something to be proud of, scrafulax or no scrafulax.

There were moral problems too, but...

I put on my first suit, folded my second suit, put it and my knives into my backpack, and took the water taxi across the bay. Scully suggested that I swim.

The Hideaway was a large, bowl-shaped terrace suspended from the trees. The kitchen itself was buried under the ground below the hanging basket of the dining room, and a dumbwaiter connected the two, sending up food and returning dirty dishes. The guests ascended to the open deck by much grander lifts that looked something like vintage rocket ships, the kind of deadly things humies from Sol's orbit used to build. Probably still do, judging from Barkbere's backwards dishwasher. He was from that part of the galaxy.

The elevator man pointed me to the kitchen entrance, which was dug into the ground. The structure of tunnels underneath was made from hard-wearing plastic, and the whole thing looked like a field kitchen that a military unit might use.

"It doesn't have to look impressive, it just has to be clean," my new chef said. He was a big Jacintha slug called Ruis who was always smiling. He was waiting for me inside the tunnel. "You're Barkbere's fireproof humie, right?" he said, laughing. I noticed a pale stick of a being hovering around behind him with a wide mop.

"Pleased to meet you," I said. "I'm Grith."

"Well, Grith, before I show you to your quarters, there's something I want you to do – this way." Chef Ruis turned his huge body and slid down the tunnel. I realised then what the mop man was for.

We entered a utilitarian and spotless kitchen.

"Everyone listen up," Ruis's voice boomed. Many eyes turned to us, although pincers, fingers and tentacles continued to work. "This is Grith, our new line cook." He handed me a blowtorch and gently pushed me forward.

I waved at them, then, keeping my hand aloft, brought the searing flame of the blowtorch up to meet it, smiling all the while. For a second, they stopped working, just for a second, then they cheered...

...and went back to work. I joined them. It was different here. There was no shouting, no cajoling, no threatening. Even in the thick of a four-hundred-cover night, there was calm in the Hideaway kitchen as Ruis called out the orders in his cheerful boom.

I worked alongside a polite broilerman called Twitch – the title just a formality since his race are hermaphrodites – and although they only had two hands, they worked as if they had four. Twitch was covered in a fine, slick fur, wore a kind of netting rather than whites, and had a rare elegance compared to the brutes and briny cranks I'd been working with.

"Watch and jump in when you can," Twitch said on my first shift. "That trick of yours will come in handy." During prep, they drew my attention to a voice-activated projector attached to the extractor hood, which cast out a recipe when given the name of a dish. I was familiar with a lot of them – glazed boater with mashed fatroots and truffles, griddled jumping jack and popping grain, fried saddle of elka, slow-cooked rockfruit – but there were slight differences to the way things were done. One dish involved capturing the fragrance of the stinking cactus oil, and serving it in a fog that wafted over the dining table. Apparently the vultures loved it.

At the end of a shift, I was sweating, breathless and glowing, but with nowhere to direct my energy. The cooks were happy with a shift well done and cleaned up to go. There was none of the high-spirited, wine-enabled messing around when Chef left that marked Barkbere's. It struck me that nobody mentioned Barkbere's, not even to me. They didn't think that they were better than us, they just didn't think about us at all.

I didn't say any of this to Barkbere or Chef when I made my first report. The three of us were crammed into the back of a delivery truck parked some distance from the coast, knees too close together, Barkbere's feelers in touching range, Chef's eyes lasering through me. There wasn't much to report. I'd seen orders of scrafulax go out, but all I knew was how it was plated – three half-shells on a plain board with a pile of grey salt from the bay on the side. Chef snorted and said nothing, arms and legs folded, except for the one without a counterpart. I'd tried looking scrafulax up in the recipe projector, but I was rarely alone in the kitchen and had to keep switching it to something else.

My other task was more successful. I borrowed the keys for the delivery entrance and the walk-in fridge from Ruis under the pretext of doing a stock check, and while I was hidden in the depths of the walk-in, I took moulds of them to give to Barkbere.

I decided to ask Twitch about scrafulax. "Dangerous, isn't it?" was my opening gambit.

"Is it?" Twitch replied with a smile.

"I heard it was poisonous."

"Salt is poisonous to a slug," they said.

I dropped it; I was too busy to talk anyway. The orders poured in and I stacked them up in my head, which was full of cooking times and a triaged to-do list. Arms, fingers, legs, tentacles and pincers moved and clicked like the parts of some great machine. Clean, efficient, elegant, we turned out the next dish and the next one, and the next. Communication was done in single words, clear and succinct over the kitchen noise, but never yelled. The kitchen and the restaurant were joined by more than just the umbilicus that took the finished dishes up to the diners. The atmosphere and attitude carried from one place to the other, from the ground to the sky and back.

Grassing to Barkbere was making me ill. I'd return to the restaurant from these meetings unable to look at anybody. Nevertheless, I continued to do my best to uncover the scrafulax secret. I helped the porter unpack deliveries of the rocky shells, and pumped him for anything he knew, which was little. I expressed interest in them to Chef Ruis: "I've never eaten one before, I heard they were really poisonous." I wheedled Twitch some more, and the other cooks too, and even the stick-like mop man, when he wasn't trailing behind Ruis.

After another fruitless clandestine meeting – Chef was seething, although he said nothing, as usual – Barkbere growled, "Scully misses you. He's looking forward to you coming back." *Coming back.* Was I really coming back? What for? As if I'd said this aloud, Barkbere added: "Chef needs a new underboss. The position is open, for now."

I went back to the Hideaway in a foul mood. My insides were churning. Underboss … that was the fast track to becoming a chef. But studying under that whispering psycho, could I manage that? I did miss Scully. I missed going fishing. But working on the line of the Hideaway was satisfying in a wholly different way, if I could bring that back with me … but I knew this wasn't possible. I was sick of the darkness – I woke up and it was dark, I worked in the false light of the kitchen all day, and when I was done, it was dark again. *How do beings live like this?*

I was making myself queasy, stirring all this inside my head, when Ruis called me over. "Hey, fireman, come here a minute, I've got something for you!" In the palm of his hand was a scrafulax, opened up, the organ gently beating inside its skin. "Tried one of these before?"

I shook my head and tried not to show how tense I was. "Is it safe?"

Ruis took the lid off a tub containing a fine, colourless powder and sprinkled it over the top. The flecks sat on the surface of the membrane then melted in. "It is now," he said, and handed it over. "Go on."

"What did you put on it?"

"My 'special dust'." He smiled. "Down in one."

I was scared of it. I looked up at the slug's smiling face and swallowed the scrafulax. It was tangy, salty, bitter. I gagged and swallowed a second time, forcing it down my throat. I felt it move in there and I choked again, my eyes watering. Ruis clapped me on the back. "Awful, aren't they?" He was laughing.

I didn't go to sleep after service. I lay awake in bed. When the noise from the bar had died, I got up, put on my suit, and bundled my second suit and knives into my backpack. Outside, it was dark again. I could see space yawning above my head, and saw the twinkle of stars millions of light years away. Goodbye, Mama. Goodbye, Papa.

I let myself into the kitchen using the set of keys that Barkbere had fabbed for me, and took a box of scrafulax from the fridge and the tub of Ruis's 'special dust'. Then I walked all the way round the coast to Barkbere's Bistro.

Barkbere woke the whole crew when I showed up. We assembled in the kitchen. Chef pried open the scrafulax and set them on the pass. I handed over the tub.

"What is it?" he whispered.

"I don't know. He called it his 'special dust'."

The vigintipede looked like he wanted to slap me with several hands at once. "Special dust?"

"It works," I said. "I've already tried it."

"How much?"

"Just a pinch."

Chef prepared them and handed them out. We stood in a loose circle: me, Barkbere, Chef, Scully, Krik, June and the other line cooks. Even the red-headed humie dishwasher was there. Barkbere obviously felt he needed to say a few words, but all he managed was, "To the future of Barkbere's Bistro!"

We swallowed them. There was a lot of choking and hacking. Even Chef couldn't keep the disgust from his face.

I was prepared, and forced mine down in one great gulp, my teeth together and mouth clamped shut, an awful taste on my tongue and a strangling sensation in my throat.

"Delicious!" Barkbere cried. His beady, flickering eyes were watering, his feelers twitching in distress. "Delicious!" He clapped me on the back with one of his great claws. "You've done it, lad, you've –"

The dishwasher vomited on the ground.

"Really," Barkbere started, "that's a terrible waste, that is one of Nilvur's, if not the galaxy's, finest delicacies and…" He trailed off as the pale, spotted humie continued to vomit and grow even paler. He heaved until blood came up and then collapsed on the floor in a pile of his own viscera.

"Is this some kind of humie thing?" Krik suggested, just before he began to puke.

"What have you done?" Chef asked. He was reaching for a knife before he too dropped, holding his guts. Barkbere was next.

The remaining cooks were looking at each other, stricken with horror. I started to back away before any of them had the sense to pick up where Chef left off. Scully was watching me. He was still standing.

"I'm sorry," I said. "I didn't mean for this to happen." Then I turned and ran.

I had only the clothes on my back when I arrived at the Hideaway. My suit was splashed with blood and bile. The look on Scully's face had followed me all the way. What had happened? Why hadn't the dust worked? My stomach was doing flip-flops, but it didn't have anything to do with the scrafulax.

Ruis was waiting for me. "You're back!" he said, jovial as ever. "How was the tasting session?" His eyes winked at the blood on my shoes.

"What happened? What did you do?"

"Nothing at all. Scrafulax is lethal in about one in four cases. I thought you knew that."

"But the dust … the special dust." I realised then how truly lame that sounded.

"Ground lice pepper. Just for flavour."

"But – but you serve it here!"

"You want to know the real secret of scrafulax, kid? The real reason beings flock to the Hideaway to try it? The risk. The thrill of it. One in four – d'you like those odds? You've eaten two already – you should be a gambling man, you've got the luck."

"Customers die here?"

"It happens, yeah, but it keeps the vultures coming back. Anyway, Barkbere's might be closed for a bit while they restaff—"

"Barkbere is dead."

"He has sons. As I was saying, you're a good line cook – Twitch agrees – and I could use you here, if you still want the job?"

I looked up at the sky: open space above the treetops, no suns, just darkness and those far-off white pinpricks that might mean life or might mean nothing at all. It was a long way home.

"I'll take it," I said.

. **Callum McSorley** is a writer based in Aberdeenshire. He graduated from the University of Strathclyde in 2013 with a degree in English, Journalism & Creative Writing, and in 2014 was selected for the Hermann Kesten Scholarship. His short stories have appeared in *Gutter, Typehouse Literary Magazine, Monstrous Regiment* and more.

As the spacecraft passed Mars and began to approach Earth, the ship's AI activated The Green Man's awakening protocol. So began 9 months, 3 weeks and 2 days of an incremental temperature rise, as well as a fractional increase in light and water levels within The Green Man's resting chamber. Oh, and the songs of Jethro Tull, Fairport Convention, and Enya on loop.

The environmental triggers were logical, of course, but not Jethro Tull. There was nothing logical about Jethro Tull.

Previously, when the AI had asked The Green Man about the songs, he had laughed wholeheartedly, agreed that the music was illogical. But, it helped to ready him and get him into the mood for encountering illogical humans once again.

The AI had been silent, busy incorporating this information into its data banks.

"You should stop and listen to it from time to time," The Green Man had said, plucking a ladybird off one of the leaves on his face and placing it on his shoulder instead. "There's something about Earth music. It's good for the soul."

"Very well," said the AI.

So in the midst of applying algorithms to the raw data obtained from the spacecraft's photometer, the AI would pause and listen to the music. And try to refrain from consigning it to oblivion.

The Green Man began to wake. He stretched his limbs and then yawned.

"How goes it?" he asked, looking around his resting chamber.

The AI, used to The Green Man's strange manner of speech, answered that all was well. "We're nearly there now."

The Green Man yawned again. "Tell me, how long ago since I was last here?"

"In Earth years, about a hundred."

"That recent?" he said.

"Yes," said the AI. "You didn't want to go too far away. You said you had 'concerns' about the planet."

"Ah yes," he said. "Now I remember. How's Earth looking?"

"I haven't got that much data. But it's hotter than it was a hundred years ago."

The Green Man sighed. "Ah well, I'd better go down and take a look."

"Where do you want me to take you?"

"To England. The county of Somerset. The last time I was there the humans were very pleased to see me. I won a prize for best fancy dress." The Green Man laughed. "I also remember a charming public house that they'd named after me."

"A public house?"

"A pub. A gathering place for the humans. At which they drink and eat. Make merry."

The Green Man was silent for a bit. "Tell me, do they still remember me? The humans. Humanity. Am I still in their consciousness?"

The AI trawled through their information network – the cloud – and found various old images and articles on The Green Man. "You're still there. Just about."

The Green Man stroked his chin, which was budding with new leaves, then toyed with one of the biome-rich acorns half-buried in his earthy skin. "Hmm. Well, give them a quick reminder."

The AI sent over more images of The Green Man.

"Did you give them my favourite likeness? The one where I'm really young?"

The AI said yes.

"Good," he said, with a smile. "It's terribly vain of me, I know. But I really like that picture."

The Green Man was silent for a bit. Slowly, he got out of his resting chamber. He walked onto the bridge and looked out of the window to see Earth, its grey moon retreating from sight. "Ah," he said, "isn't it beautiful."

"It's rather like your own planet," said the AI, "from what I recall."

The Green Man nodded. "It is. Maybe that's why I'm so fond of it."

"Will you help them, the humans? If they've damaged it beyond repair?"

"Maybe," said The Green Man. "Maybe not. It depends."

He toyed again with one of the acorns on his face. "These are precious. And not to be given away on a whim."

The AI brought up the latest data from the photometer, gave The Green Man a large figure for the number of planets transiting a star.

"That's got bigger."

"Yes. We've still got many planets to visit. Though some of them won't be habitable. So," said the AI, suddenly curious, "why bother with Earth?"

The Green Man exhaled deeply.

"I mean," the AI went on, "if the humans are stupid enough to destroy their own planet, why help them? And anyway, one day their sun will die."

"I know," said The Green Man. "And I'd have to call in a lot of favours to reverse that."

The AI considered this for a fraction of a millisecond. "Favours? What do you mean?"

The Green Man laughed, "I'd have to visit an old flame – a crotchety beauty even older than me. Sweet talk her. Though God only knows where she is nowadays. I wonder if she still lives in that house with the chicken legs."

"An old flame?" said the AI. If it could've been round-eyed it would have been. "I have never fully understood your life cycle – I have too little data from your species – but is a female involved?"

The Green Man grinned. "Sometimes, sometimes not. But for my biomes to thrive, and for me to have a long life, yes, a female is necessary."

The Green Man suddenly took on a faraway look as he remembered some of his past loves. "Chernila," he muttered. "I miss her stories. And the sirens. Their music was..." The Green Man paused, lost in memories.

The AI looped back to its earlier question. "But why Earth?"

The Green Man, his reverie broken, shrugged. "Because."

"Because why?"

"Because of the forests."

They both fell silent. The Green Man suddenly laughed. "And Jethro Tull *does* make excellent music."

The AI sputtered out a string of numbers. It was its way of giving vent to its thoughts. A brain fart, as it were.

The Green Man smiled. "You didn't like the Jethro Tull?"

"No."

"Give it some time," said The Green Man. "Give it some time."

Teika Marija Smits is the pen-name of Dr Teika Bellamy, a UK-based writer, artist, editor and ex-scientist. Her writing has appeared in various places including *Mslexia, Brittle Star, Strix, LossLit* and *Literary Mama.*
When she's not busy with her children, or creating, she's managing the indie press, Mother's Milk Books. https://marijasmits.wordpress.com/

Lulu Laguna

Tiffany Meuret

The club was full of many things – throaty music and booze and people carrying on like carefree idiots. As it should be, considering the pall that descended upon them every night at closing. Best to enjoy these last few minutes.

Observing her namesake from the upper deck, Lu counted the sea of scalps in search of one in particular. Cigarette smoke curled around her, hanging low like a fog. Lulu Laguna wasn't a big place, nothing but a dance floor, a closet with a toilet, and a bar. A sliver of walkway, which they called the upper deck (for no other reason than it sounded classy as hell) ran in the rafters.

The scalp she sought stopped dancing and turned to face her. It was as if they didn't need words anymore. It'd been a long time since words had been of any use anyway.

Troy was her partner. He'd helped found the club, lived with her, fucked her on occasion when the stars aligned, and generally hung around to irritate the shit out of her. This had been her dream and, by proxy, his too. Their morbid, fucked-up dream.

Closing time rapidly approached. Like her, Troy felt it in his bones. Every night for the last however long – their biological clocks ticked towards midnight, resetting at a second past, doomed to repeat for the rest of their lives.

Lu watched him climb the ladder to meet her on the upper deck. His clogs slipped on the rungs – heinous fucking shoes.

"Care to dance?" Troy asked upon reaching her. He ran a bangled arm across his forehead, wiping away the sweat.

She blew smoke in his face. "I'd rather die."

"You've dressed for such an occasion, I see."

She was nothing if not prepared for any occasion. Her clothing was multipurpose, with lots of pockets for knick-knacks and airline bottles. Troy despised her cargo pants and she despised his clogs, but they wore them anyway. Probably out of spite.

"Need space for my cigarettes."

He leaned over the rail, gazing at the sprawling party below him. "Where is Shakes?"

Lu motioned toward the door. He was ready. Everyone was ready. Shakes had been with them since the first year, however long ago that was. All the booze and blow really took a toll on the long term memory.

Troy rubbed his lips together, like he always did when he was nervous. After all this time, it still made him nervous. Every night. Every time. Lu had to remind herself that it was a good thing that he still hated it as much as he did. It kept the rest of them human.

"That's Peter," he said, pointing towards a person she didn't bother to look at. "He choked on his tequila shot earlier. Threw up all over the bar. Never tried the stuff before, but he says he can't wait to do it again. I told Menny to cut him off."

"Why?" It wasn't like Menny listened to anything they said anyway. Well, she didn't listen to anything Troy said, mostly.

"I don't know. It was like watching a kid trying on their parent's clothes. Trying to look all grown and distinguished, when they're really just terrified children."

"But they aren't children. They're fucking adults. If they want to get wasted, let them get wasted."

Troy faced her. "Not Peter. He wouldn't have liked it. He'd have been scared."

"He doesn't have enough time to be scared. None of them do. That's the point."

Troy looked down at the top of Peter's head, which was already starting to droop.

"Always one of the first to go. I wonder why that is?"

Lu shrugged. It was impossible to know. The facility was never supposed to exist in the first place. When it all went to shit after a couple of clandestine decades, the records – if there ever were any – were destroyed. The only way to know for sure was to walk down there and snoop around. She was still waiting on the few that had tried to return.

"Peters always make such a fucking mess."

"They can't help it."

Exhaling towards the ladder, she stamped out her cigarette on the handrail. "Doesn't mean I have to like it."

Troy clicked the bangles on his arm. *Clink clink clink*. Twelve total. "Is it midnight yet?"

"Thirty seconds, thereabouts." She lit another cigarette.

A woman dropped to the floor below them, knees giving out. A Sandy or a Layla, it was difficult to tell. A few others hoisted her up by her elbows, assuming her to be a tad too drunk or a tad too high instead of a tad too dead. They wouldn't have time to figure it out.

Midnight struck. The music cut, silence crashing through the room. The dance floor froze as all the bodies crumpled, slapping tile and cracking skulls as they did. The trigger was silent, but Lu swore she could hear it anyway – the scramble of code that fried the implants embedded in the brains of all those dancers. Clones. All of them. Clones on the verge of expiring, straddling the thin line between mild confusion and catastrophic degradation. Clones with nowhere else to go. Besides the facility itself, Lulu Laguna was the only living, breathing place within fifteen miles.

Midnight struck, plus fifteen seconds, and everyone besides herself, Troy, Menny, and Shakes, was dead. Some of the clones twitched as their nerves misfired, but by 12:01 that usually stopped.

Troy was already halfway down the ladder, losing a shoe along the way. It landed in a puddle of vomit. "Oh god damn it."

"They're stupid shoes," Lu said.

"They're *great* shoes."

It had been a busy night, and there were at least thirty bodies to remove between the four of them. Shakes already had the dolly ready and was stacking people like bags of sand. Lu's glove caught on fire from one of her cigarettes. Troy jingled as he worked, his startling strength put to good use as he swaggered across the club with a body flung over each shoulder. Menny counted and categorized, scratching notes that made little sense to anybody but her.

They worked through the night, not stopping until the floor was cleared.

Lu squatted outside her front door, watching the scraped earth space where the clones had been tagged, piled, and later removed by canvas-flapped cargo Humvees. Depending on the day, she was either just up or still up, yet watched it all the same. There wasn't much else to do here anyway, and they weren't due for a trip to Sand Town for another six days.

The facility blocked out the morning sun, casting a fat shadow that reached damn near to her toes, despite its distance. It was built out here on purpose, on the vestigial rim of a podunk town whose last whiff of industry stemmed from the first transcontinental railroad and, later, prickly pear jelly that was canned out of someone's bathtub and sold at the tow yard. They called it Sand Town because that was all a person could reliably find there.

The four of them each had their own yurt-like home, plopped haphazardly in the desert space behind the club. Troy snored through the walls of her tiny home, having inconsiderately slept in her bed the previous night. They often shared a bed, for the sake of familiarity more than anything, flip-flopping between homes based on whichever of them left Lulu Laguna first.

Hidden more carefully, with exceptional care to avoid outside detection lest they be confiscated, were the graves. Troy and Lu marked theirs with shadows, fastening all sorts of kitschy shit they'd collected in Sand Town to Lu's yurt. Precisely at sunrise, the shadows those items cast pointed to the individual graves. A ceramic frog, a shattered flower pot, a dream catcher, a wind chime – only they knew where the bodies were buried. Menny and Shakes had their own graves, but Lu didn't know where, and she'd never ask.

The snoring ceased, and Lu knew it was time to go inside and get some proper sleep, or else Troy would pitch a fit and make that impossible. His compulsive worrying over her health was one of the most crushing aspects of the whole affair. He'd tried once to get her to quit smoking, going so far as to burn all her cigarettes in the chimenea out back. She'd tried to punch him in the face. His new thing was assigning her rigorous sleep schedules.

Her sleep was haunted, as usual.

The night started slow. Music pulsed off the walls, thrashed at all the senses. Some nights it was just the four of them drinking alone at the bar, craning their heads towards the door at every squeak of a barstool, every sneeze and cough and extra loud gulp (Troy). They never wanted any guests, really, but ached for them all the same. What if it was one of theirs? Their friend, their lover, their child? To recognize anyone was a rarity nowadays. After so many years in the game, either the stock of clones was waning, or the facility had employed some other nefarious way to dispatch them. The four of them were hunters, so to speak, but that wasn't why any of them were there.

No one really understood just what had happened at that place. Equally inscrutable was why it hadn't been burned to the ground and blamed on terrorists, like every other devious product of war. Things were so disorganized that disoriented clones were washing up on the shores of civilized society, going insane and attacking people. There was an uproar – a brief lament and demand for change before Lu and her cohorts were employed by the facility's PR team, and then the clones' stories collected cobwebs in the face of a thousand more easily accessible atrocities.

Troy toyed with his bangles, each lovingly crafted by hand with pliable steel that he'd ordered via their monthly cost-of-living stipend. Lu had her cigarettes. Menny had her booze. Shakes had his books.

The three were accustomed to long bouts of shared silence, except when Troy bitched incessantly.

"I have a blister," he said, rubbing his ankle.

Lu scoffed. "You have issues."

"Liking shoes is not an issue, bitch."

"Liking bad shoes is."

He lunged for the skin under her bicep, looking to pinch her because she hated it, but she slapped his hand away. "Slow days are the worst."

Menny nodded in agreement, wiping the dry counter for the fifth time in twenty minutes. Shakes never said much at all.

"I wish we could turn the music off. No one's here anyway," Troy said.

No one responded. They all knew that wasn't an option. The music was their lure, the bass drumming at the ground attracted desperate humans better than words or signs or arrows etched in the dirt. Music didn't lie. Everyone knew what they were in for – or thought they did.

The door swung open, then closed. Shakes left. He often retreated to his yurt on slow days, returning the moment a guest appeared as if smelling their arrival.

Lu rested her palm on Troy's shoulder. "Just go home. I'll come get you if we need you."

Troy nodded, but didn't get up.

The door opened. It was Shakes again.

Menny slapped her rag on the counter. "Damn it, Shakes. Pick one. In or out."

He dropped his head to one side, indignant at the thought that he would do anything to waste his own time. "Someone is coming."

The way he said it, the way he bored holes into them with his stare, it meant he recognized that someone.

Troy choked on his drink. It'd been months since one of their own had arrived at the club. A mixture of anticipation and dread filled the room, each of them praying that it was someone they knew and also that it wasn't. Because after the initial the joy settled they'd have to watch their loved one die. Again.

Shakes meandered to the bar, dropping a hand on Lu's forearm. Fuck.

Letting out a series of breathy denunciations, Troy sprung up. "Okay. Alright. Oh Jesus, but…yeah, it's going to be fine. Right Lu? Wegotthisitwillbejustfine."

"Yeah," she said, eyes not leaving the door. "Just fine, buddy."

The woman – Lu and Troy's special someone – entered mere moments later. She was alone and dressed in the same white cotton tunic as the rest of them. Her feet were caked in desert, cheeks flushed. Her hair was longer than most clones', almost down to her ass, still just as ink-black as Lu remembered. She looked so young.

She *was* young.

Like all twelve times before, Lu resisted the urge to run at her, snatch her into her embrace and never let her go. Instead, she nodded, raising a glass, exhaling a storm of smoke.

"Join us, Ophelia," Lu said.

Clink clink clink. Menny produced three fresh glasses like a bartending machine. The drinks were poured – neat whiskey for Lu and Troy, and one seltzer water – before Ophelia had taken a step.

Despite being clones, the initial moments never played out the same, varying based on the nuance of the room. Their condition, too, varied. Sometimes dirty, sometimes scared, sometimes dehydrated, sometimes pissed and in shock. The mélange of human emotion never ceased to surprise.

This Ophelia did not ask how Lu knew her name or who they all were or what even was in the drink. She simply slid onto the nearest stool to Lu, threw back the glass and chugged.

"Hm," Ophelia said. "That's all?"

Menny poured another whiskey, sliding it to Ophelia.

Troy eyed them all, unconsciously running a finger through his bangles.

Shakes posted himself by the door, where he would remain until midnight. They had six hours.

Reunited again, the trio hunched over their drinks, Ophelia wincing through the sting of the alcohol. "I never liked whiskey much."

Menny paused her relentless scrubbing, arching a brow towards Ophelia. "That so?"

Ophelia replied with an acuteness most clones lack, more than even her own former selves. "Don't worry, Menny. It's still my drink of choice."

Troy dropped his drink. Lu soaked up a deep pull of nicotine, staring at Ophelia's foggy silhouette through the oozing smoke.

"Well," Lu said. "What have we here?"

Ophelia faced her, lips hiding a smirk. "You know what we have."

"Of course I know. My question is, how the fuck do you?"

"I'm a clone, not stupid."

None of the other Ophelias had done this. None of them ever knew they were clones before being told.

Troy siphoned the liquor from his glass with abandon, Menny always on the ready with a refill. Lu couldn't hear anything beyond the roar of adrenaline-fueled blood rushing through her ears, couldn't see anything beyond the curvature of Ophelia's slender back, the algae-green of her eyes. "How long have you been awake?"

She shrugged, dragging a finger over the rim of her glass. "Not long."

"Liar."

Ophelia smiled, but her eyes remained dark.

Six hours. "You have an implant?" She wasn't even sure why she asked, as if Ophelia would have any way of knowing the absolute truth.

"I presume."

Six hours.

Lu finished her drink. Another appeared. Clutching the glass in one hand and a shaky cigarette in the other, she motioned for the door, turning a glance over one shoulder to Troy. "Shall we?"

Ophelia paused, the glass rim at her lips. "What's in this, anyway?"

"Whiskey."

Hesitating a moment longer, she finished it in a single pull. "Liar."

Lu felt her colleagues' eyes running up and down her back as she shuttled Ophelia away, Troy following them like a confused shadow. His anxiety infected the room, but Lu was used to that by now.

Pointing the way to her yurt, Lu studied Ophelia's familiar frame as she stopped to inspect one of the windchimes near the front door – a cactus with a series of small bells dangling from its appendages. "This is hideous," Ophelia said, smiling.

At this affront, Troy set aside his nerves in favor of a proper callout. "I'll have you know that this—" He pointed toward the cactus "—is a *priceless* handicraft."

"I'm sure it is," she said. "Priceless, I mean." Reaching out to touch it, she pulled her hand back into the folds of her arms, trying to hide her trembling.

Glaring at Troy from over Ophelia's shoulder, Lu opened the front door. "Have a seat if you want."

Ophelia did not, instead sticking to the walls, shoulders rounded to fit against the slope of the dome.

"Or not. Whatever."

Lu blunted the end of her cigarette just to fire up another. Yet each new cig was a disappointment, because it was no different than the last. There was always that hope, though, that she might get lucky. Even if just once.

Her living arrangements were nothing more than bare white walls, a plastic bedside table, and a bed pushed to one end, covers draped over the edge and melting on the floor. The three of them stood an arm's-length away from each other – the farthest they could manage in such a small space. Lu's smoke sulked around the room, casting a grey haze over their faces.

Ophelia began, chipping away at the silence. "I take it it's been a while since we've seen each other."

"It has."

"It probably never gets any easier, does it?"

Troy's expression was grim, and he studied Lu's every move with his arms crossed, their roles reversed in this new space, as if the jitters that plagued him in the club wouldn't fit in this smaller room. All of them were professional emotional packers – they'd learned to leave certain feelings outside when necessary.

"How do you know so much?" he asked.

Uncrossing herself, then changing her mind, she shifted her weight to her other hip.

Lu polished off her drink. "Well?"

"I read it."

Troy snorted, despite himself. "Read what?"

"Your file."

Hovering between the women, he said, "Bullshit."

But Ophelia was never one to lie. It was beneath even her clone. "Hey O? When's my birthday?"

"September twenty-fifth," she said, firing it off without a blink. "Troy's?"

"March first."

"Yours?"

Leaning against the wall, she exhaled long and heavy. "September too. Just before yours."

"Psh," Troy said. "That doesn't prove anything."

But it did, and he knew it.

They could go on all night, Ophelia rattling off fact after fact about their lives, whatever shit was collected on them, whatever information was inside said 'file'. Clone Ophelia would know it all, because, just like the original, she possessed the most magnificent photographic memory. Lu always figured that's how she got recruited in the first place. They'd done studies on her, doctors and psychologists and all sorts of people professing all the things they would do just to spend but a moment inside her head.

Most of the time, Lu felt the same way.

Lu, Troy, and Ophelia had all been friends, but it was the women that fashioned an ironclad bond, one that Troy sometimes (all times) resented. Not because of what they were or who they were or even because he wasn't involved, but because he had had eyes for just one of them, and she had had eyes for only Lu.

When O arrived those other twelve times, Troy had clung to the walls, cloaked himself in Lu's smoke and agony, and let the moment be. He watched like he always had – from the places darkened by their bodies, the shadows that they made as they held one another.

He helped her bury her. He held Lu's hand. He was a better person than she deserved, who also enjoyed ugly shoes a little too much.

They stood around for a while, saying nothing, until it became clear that Ophelia could no longer hide her shaking. It was Troy that led O to the bed to sit down, and it was Troy that guided Lu beside her.

"What the hell is in that drink?" O asked, her body darkening ever slightly to the unnatural color of a bruise.

"Relaxers. Opiates."

"That explains it." Ophelia hated to lose control. The thought of it attacked her body like an allergy. "They're still there, you know. Working. There are dozens more of me. I saw them. The file was up on the screen as I woke up, just left there for me to see. They knew I'd read it. They knew I'd come here. They know what I'm telling you."

O's cheek was sticky and cold, but Lu held her palm there anyway. She'd heard bits of it before, whatever broken amounts the other Os had pieced together.

"They're watching you too," Ophelia said.

"They pay my fucking salary, dearest. They've watched every shit, every sob, every fuck, every everything."

Ophelia rested her head in the crook of Lu's arm. Troy whirred about in the background, bundling up blankets from the floor into his arms. Preparing.

"Then what the hell are you doing here?"

"I don't know," Lu said, more smoke escaping her mouth than words. "No matter how many times we get you back, we never get the answers we want. The answer *I* want. There isn't any reason to it at all."

Troy sat on the opposite side of the bed, bundling the blankets behind him. "Why are you here, O? Knowing what you know? I mean, why even bother? It's not like you remember us. Or remember Lu."

It should have stung Lu to hear such a thing, but it didn't. She was wondering about it herself.

"Even ghosts need closure."

They lay together, the three of them, Troy and Lu recalling stories of their past to this new Ophelia. She laughed at their jokes even though they'd told them to her twelve other times. They answered the same questions despite twelve other answers. They took turns brushing hands to her forehead and cheeks as her warmth siphoned away. The clones that made it to them were always very fragile, death gaining on them faster than they could run. Their existence wasn't sustainable, but that didn't seem to matter to the people in charge of creating them. And until the investors decided to use their millions to fund a different cloak-and-dagger method of destruction, Lu would be here, and Ophelia would come.

Midnight struck. The music died, and so did O.

Nobody cried.

They buried her at dawn.

The desert was bare and flat, shrubbery snuffed out by the constant piling of bodies. The Humvees had come and gone. It had been three weeks since O's last visit.

Troy stalked out his front door, finishing off a yawn with a good scratching of his ass. He'd slept at his place and Lu at hers for twenty-one days.

Instinct carried him to her, perhaps sensing something in the way she leaned toward him, the way her eyes narrowed as she studied him. Or maybe he was just tired of sleeping like shit, having been used to another breathing person sharing his bed all these years.

He motioned for the cigarette in her hand, which she offered without complaint. Stealing a long drag, he said nothing as smoke poured out of him.

"It might not have always been," Lu said. "But now, it's you."

Ash floated to the dirt beneath his feet as he flicked the cigarette between his fingers. "These things taste like shit."

On impulse, she grabbed him by the neck, pulling him into a kiss. "Tastes fine to me." The moment was brief, but enough.

He returned her cigarette, and they went to work.

Tiffany Meuret is a born and raised desert dweller hailing from Phoenix, Arizona. Her work has been published or is forthcoming from *MoonPark Review, Martian, Ellipsis Zine, Collective Unrest,* and others. Find her on Twitter @TMeuretBooks. Be prepared for passionate discussions on coffee and pocket-sized dogs.

A Crest of a Wave

Tim Major

Below the carriage, the surface of Mars glistened crystalline in the dawn light. Liss Crowther pressed her forehead against the window, trying to ignore the sand-streaks that marked the clear plastic. The carriage shuddered, the engines straining to keep the small capsule level and stationary.

"Can't we get going?" Liss's wife, Marian, lay back in her contoured seat, her eyes closed. "It's too early. I'm still asleep. The least you can do is get me to a hotel."

"One sec," Liss said. She narrowed her eyes and the transport lanes below became threads of gold, the headlights of carriages spaced at regular intervals like fairy lights. Reluctantly, she turned from the window. "Okay. So where do you fancy?"

Marian opened one eye. "Seriously? I assumed you were whisking me away. Isn't that how anniversaries work?"

Liss took her hand. "Didn't we agree in our vows to be equal? Facing our future side by side, or some such. I hired the carriage, didn't I?"

Marian shrugged. "Fair enough. So, let's see…" She lapsed into silent thought.

Liss's eyes travelled to the window on Marian's side of the carriage. The vast city of Tharsis Foxglove had the appearance of an exotic snail, the swirls of its central mound spiralling towards the sharp apex of its uppermost parliament buildings. The thin tower stakes that marked its original perimeter had thinned, worn by sand. The suburbs had crept further outwards in the decades since the city had settled here, never again to roam the deserts of Mars.

"I'm so sick of it," Marian said. "The city, I mean. Let's get away. And I don't mean the Daisychains or even Tharsis Primrose, heaven forbid. That place is all geared towards families these days."

Liss's fingers spasmed, gripping her hand tightly for a moment. Marian appeared not to notice.

Marian tapped her front teeth with a blue-painted nail. "We've pretty much covered the foothills, and I bet you didn't pack our boots anyway. Let's go to the old coast. That'd be a dramatic way to commemorate our wedding."

Liss gave a doubtful look. "Isn't it falling apart? Erosion?"

Marian prodded her lightly in the ribs. "I assume you're referring to the coast, not our marriage."

Responding to Liss's spoken command, the carriage slid down into the traffic canal and shrugged into forward motion, its shiver becoming a smooth sway.

The carriage settled in the centre of a public square. Its huffing retrojets glossed the cobbles with fog that quickly vanished in the chill morning air. Liss exited the vehicle first, then turned to help Marian down.

Only the sound of the distant wind punctuated the calm. The air here remained still, the wind scooped up and away by the sand-sculpted barrier that they had passed moments before the carriage's descent.

"This place has seen better days," Liss said. She spun slowly on her heel. Shabby hotels surrounded the square, their painted facades wrinkled and worn. Metal tables and chairs spilled out from one lobby, as if creeping towards the centre of the square. Among the overturned café furniture Liss noticed a few high chairs and playpens for children.

"Happy days," Marian said.

"You've been here before?"

"When I was a kid. It was heaven. Tacky, sure, but heaven all the same." She pointed to a hotel opposite the café. One strut of the lobby awning had collapsed, depositing chunky lettering onto the ground. Only a large letter X remained attached, a warning against entry. "That's where we always stayed. The Excelsior. There was an ice-cube machine on every floor. Me and Kip had corridor ice-fights each night before bed."

"I can't remember the last time you talked about your childhood."

Marian spun to face her. "I can't remember a day when you didn't."

Liss rubbed at her cheek with the sleeve of her woollen dress.

"Sorry," Marian said. "It's just—"

Liss interrupted. "Which way's the seafront?"

They passed through the tatty streets, avoiding the rents in the paving. Instinctively, Liss found herself keeping to the centre of each street, fearing for the stability of the buildings towering above them. The street opened into a wide promenade, bordered by a flaking white barrier running the length of the walkway.

Liss gasped. "Good grief. Is that the sea?"

The waves appeared far too high and too close, as if they might envelope the promenade in a matter of moments. The crest of the largest wave curled down into itself like a fern. Liss gripped the white barrier to steady herself and to provide a measure of scale.

"It's beautiful," Marian said.

"Shouldn't it be moving?"

Marian smiled. "It did, once. The last time I was here, in fact, but that was more than twenty years ago. The crash of the waves was incredible. I've no idea how it worked."

Liss peered at the enormous wave, trying to discern the trick. Now she saw that the wave glinted brown like the sand-sculpted buildings of the early settlements. A thin rain of dust dripped from its tip, forming sand hills below the crest. "Some sort of reiterating terraform tech, I guess. Constantly renewing in subtly different formations."

"Bluffer."

"Come on," Liss said, tugging at Marian's arm, "I'll buy you an ice cream."

The seafront shops had been long abandoned and they met nobody on their journey along the promenade. The extent of the disrepair became more evident the further they walked. A Victorian-style bandstand lay tilted, sunk into the ground with paving slabs turned ninety degrees to ease its passage. It must be a consequence of the terraformed sand having become brittle over the years, but Liss found it difficult to shake the image of the sand wave having once burst from the ocean to flood the ground, softening the foundations of the small building. She hoped it was only her imagination that made the cobbles beneath her feet seem porous and yielding.

She moved to stand between Marian and the sand sea. "This isn't working out."

Marian pulled a face. "You're breaking up with me, on our anniversary?"

"Funny. Come on, this was a bad idea. Let's go to the Daisychains after all. There might be space in the spa."

"But it's all so *fake*," Marian said.

Liss gestured with a thumb over her shoulder. "And, in contrast, this is all perfectly natural, is it?"

"It is, now that it's been left for dead. There's nothing more natural than decay."

When had this begun, this morbidity, this fixation on the past and the dying? As they walked side by side, Liss's hands clenched and unclenched as she rehearsed possible conversations with their traps and dead-ends. But it was impossible to concentrate on future plans, surrounded by sand-sculpted edifices of the past. Perhaps that was Marian's intention, bringing them here.

The promenade split into two. The first path led to a wrought-iron gateway, but the pier beyond had long since disintegrated. Liss turned towards the second path, which bent back towards the town, but Marian placed a restraining hand on her arm. She pointed ahead to a dilapidated building that crouched between the pier entrance and the neighbouring hotels. Its corrugated-metal walls contrasted against the stonework of the other buildings. A neon sign flickered on the rusted porch. *Museum of automata and the past*. Underneath, the words *OPEN* and *CLOSED* lit one at a time, in turn.

Marian strode to the door and pushed it ajar before Liss could protest. Liss paused, glanced at the static, curled crest of the sand wave, then followed.

Dim recessed lamps lit the lobby of the museum. Marian stood before a desk that held a cash till. Pencil lines divided an open visitors' book into columns. The few rows of entries were faded and illegible.

"There's nobody here," Liss said.

Marian picked up a gold bell from beside the till. Its sharp tinkle echoed around the space.

They waited. Nobody came.

"Do you think we should leave any payment?" Marian said.

"I think we should leave, full stop."

"Grow some balls, Liss."

Marian's hand pushed gently at the base of Liss's spine, shoving her through the velveteen curtain that masked the first doorway leading from the lobby. The room was wider than the front of the building had suggested, its centre open and empty like an art gallery. Instead of paintings, figures lined each wall in huddled groups. Liss pushed backwards against Marian's arm.

"It's okay," Marian whispered, "They're just aye-ayes. There's no one here."

The robots had been dressed in human clothing, fixed in tableaux depicting domestic scenes. The first group of four aye-ayes wore thick winter clothing. Two had been arranged as if in the act of constructing a man from the cotton snow. In the foreground, another couple stood side by side, arm in arm, their blank faces turned towards each other as if kissing mid-stride.

At the far wall a tuxedoed robot knelt before a standing figure wearing a thin dress that fluttered in the slight breeze produced by Liss and Marian's arrival. The arms of the kneeling robot made a raised triangle. If it had hands they might have been clasped, but, like all of the other aye-ayes, its arms were truncated. The control-stems at the ends of its arms flickered blue, faintly.

In the final scene two robots stood at the back of the setting, both heads tilted to gaze down at a smaller figure. This half-size aye-aye appeared frozen in the act of unwrapping a gift box almost as large as itself. On a low table beside the dwarf robot, fake candles twinkled on a plastic cake.

"I hate it," Liss said. "Please, let's go?" She turned away and tried to distract herself by reading the notices beside the doorway. *Are you a fourth-gen settler or later? Do you have stories of Earth? Talk to Desmond to preserve your memories in our repertoire.*

Marian knelt before the birthday tableau, her head tilted to inspect the face of the crouching aye-aye.

"I've never seen one this size," she said. "What a weird idea."

She reached out to the robot. As her hand passed before its control-stem arms, it lurched into jerky motion. Marian rocked back onto her haunches, startled. The aye-aye's arms waved like a sleepwalker, inches from the gift box. The wrapping slipped downwards, perhaps tugged by unseen threads. Marian laughed.

Liss's voice, when she found it, was hoarse. "Get away from it. Now. *Now*, Mal."

Marian turned. "What's wrong? There's no danger. It's just a show."

"Stop this! I'm not talking about danger. Stop torturing me."

Marian's face paled. She edged away from the child robot.

"I mean, you won't even discuss it," Liss continued, unable to stop the words spilling from her mouth. "You know how simple it is these days. Just a single trip to the surgery for implantation. You know it'd be me doing it, not you. You value your body too much, and that's okay. I'd care for it, too. I could do it."

Marian stood before her, hovering inches away like the child aye-aye and its mysterious gift. "If it's so simple, if you need me so little, why don't you just go ahead and have it?"

"Because—" emotion clogged Liss's throat, "—I want it to be *our* decision."

Marian glanced again at the half-size robot. It continued gesticulating towards the box which wrapped and unwrapped itself slowly. Without meeting Liss's eye, she slipped out of the room.

Liss swayed, sobbing. Around her, the tableaus creaked into motion. The faces of the winter walkers met with a dull tink. The tuxedoed robot raised its arms in a gesture of supplication. The parents of the child aye-aye drew closer together, expressing joy despite their blank plastic faces. Liss quickly withdrew from the room, pulling the curtains closed behind her.

She passed through the empty lobby to find Marian in a second curtained chamber. Far smaller and dimmer than the first, this room contained less humanoid robots, earlier models that Liss recognised only from textbooks about the development of aye-ayes back on Earth. Most of them were only torsos and heads mounted on plinths, their blank faces raised to eye height. These models were designed to perform specialised tasks: write work performance reviews, select music based on external indicators of mood, diary confidants.

Marian stood before the head and shoulders of an aye-aye partially draped in a patterned cloth. Golden zodiac symbols dotted its black plinth.

"I remember," she said quietly. "I remember this one. It's supposed to be a fortune-teller. But it turned out that the process was more impressive than the result. It scans the user, looking for signs and indicators of mood and personality. An old cold-reading trick, but automated and reliable. They rebranded it as The Empathiser, capable of mimicking any user."

Liss hung back. "I don't care. You're stuck in the past, Mal. I'm tired of hearing about it. I want to think about what's next for us. I want to at least talk about it. Are we never going to be a family, for real?"

Marian reached out to the plinth to press the single grey button. The head of the aye-aye tilted vertically, its blue eyes travelling up and down Marian's body, dwelling on her face. Her cheeks glistened.

The aye-aye turned its attention towards Liss.

"I'm really, really sorry." It was the aye-aye that spoke, but despite the tinniness of its voice, Liss recognised the inflections of Marian's own vocal patterns. A clever mimicry indeed. Liss glanced to her wife, but Marian had retreated a step into the dark.

"I love you," the aye-aye said.

"Stop this," Liss said, unsure whether to address the aye-aye or Marian herself.

The aye-aye's head tilted downwards. Liss imagined the blush that would have made it unmistakeably Marian's gesture. Its blue irises dilated and its head jerked left and right slightly, as if it was surprised to discover the truncation of its body below the shoulders.

Haltingly, it said, "I don't know how to explain myself."

For a few moments more it stared at its zodiac plinth, neck stretched so that if it had possessed a body it would have been looking down at it.

Then the aye-aye's eyes raised. Its gaze met Liss's, and then they both turned to look at Marian's belly.

Tim Major lives in York. His SF novel *Snakeskins* will be published by Titan Books in 2019; other forthcoming books include a YA novel and a short story collection. Tim's short stories have appeared in *Interzone, Best of British Science Fiction* and *Best Horror of the Year*. www.cosycatastrophes.com

The Lecture

E.M. Faulds

Lecture 8 Module 2: Assessing Wendamagan cultural values through their artefacts.

We discovered this object in amongst a great amount of low-value debris. It took our conservators quite a while to repair it, but when we got it working – the look of surprise on our faces – it started playing music!

Of course, we weren't at all sure that it was music at first as it was so, aha, alien to us. But after careful study, we can confidently state that this is certainly a musical replaying device.

And not only that, but it is filled with an astounding number of distinct pieces! Although at times it was very difficult for us to distinguish one song from another – because whereas we view music as a very individual mode of self-expression, for the culture that dominated this region, *uniformity* seems to have had greater worth.

Perhaps it's true, as some commentators have posited, that music as an art form was just not valued by them in the same way that we do. Quantity certainly trumps quality for the Wendamagans!

But we shouldn't judge this society based on our own cultural norms. What does an object like this tell us, really, about their societal values? Not much in isolation.

Although music indicates a degree of sophisticated thought, we do have to take into account other artefacts from their Pre-Catastrophe period to get a clearer picture. Case in point, this lantern object was found on a lower stratigraphy, but in such abundance, that it must have been universally familiar. Most were broken and it wasn't until we found one intact and powered it up that we discovered its true nature. As a lantern – per se – the level of light is insufficient for most indoor chores. But once it gets going, something rather extraordinary happens. The liquid contained in the inner chamber – you will note – has two different densities and colourful globules travel up and down, like so.

The point of it remains a mystery. It's quite a hypnotic effect, I'm sure you'll agree, and that leads us to believe it had a place in their spiritual life, perhaps adding a trance effect to shamanic rituals. The coincidence of intoxicant materials and primitive drum-like instruments in the same deposits certainly shows an "altered state" was needed for full appreciation of this "globule-trance-lamp"!

But – and I can't stress this enough – the rituals of a society are hard to evaluate when looked at through the prism of our own subjective viewpoint.

This, for example, is a projectile weapon designed to do violence on another. Despite its crude mechanism, it is perfectly designed for one of their hands, and – underneath the corrosion – it was once highly polished, indicating a degree of aesthetic value, despite its deadly purpose.

As some other commentators have suggested, perhaps as with music, life was simply not valued. Their population was practically killing their planet. Perhaps a cavalier attitude to life was an evolutionary mechanism just to clear some space!

As unpalatable as this is, is it wrong?

Evidence from the bone record shows that some castes had a much harder life than others, and this is proven by the malnutrition and disease markers found. Residue scrapings from cookpots indicate a diet devoid of important nutrients but high in simple carbohydrates, which is a sign in any type of fauna of a precarious existence. These all point to neglect, perhaps even slavery being endemic. Certainly, some kind of coercion would have been necessary to keep these groups in line. Perhaps the artefacts I have shown you were a way to encourage compliance from the lower social strata.

But again, it's difficult to know. The discipline of xeno-archaeology is still new. The more we study this extinct species, the more we begin to understand that despite their brief and savage existence, we share a common being-ness.

We can only hope that during our colonisation process of Wendamagan, as we cleanse and reform the planet, we will not repeat the mistakes of these poor people.

Thank you.

E.M. Faulds is an Australian who lives in Scotland. Her science fiction novel, *Ada King*, is available on Amazon now, and she helms a podcast, *Speculative Spaces*, where she interviews other speculative fiction creators – with a Scottish twist. She makes flippant tweets under the handle @BethKesh.

Full Contact

D. A. D'Amico

Kahikahea **lost the platform** when the nearest oko lumbered out of position, blocking her line of sight. It crashed into a divot on the ridge ahead, but the oko hadn't noticed. They never did.

She swore. Her fingers trembled in their worn gauntlets, and she tried to calm herself. Anger would use up more air than quiet resignation, she reminded herself. She'd have to wait until they got back to Earth before she could stomp and scream and rage without fretting over her O_2 consumption.

"I didn't think that'd work anyway," she mumbled as she watched the oko lumber away on an elongated foot-muscle, undulating through the canyon-sized channel far below.

It moved with glacial slowness, as big as a fifty-storey building. Cascading shades of blue outlined its dumbbell-shaped outer tegument. Mountainous flesh billowed like a sail caught in a strong breeze as it moved, turning as rigid as a wall of ice with every pause, while a spaghetti of appendages swirled medusa-like from its triangular head.

"I give up." Captain Manolo Castel threw his hands in the air, his voice holding all the tension Kahikahea felt. His orange pressure suit, with its faded patches and scraped, dented helmet, made him look small against the landscape of riotous color.

"I can't surrender. *I* want to live." Kahikahea shared his frustration. She wanted nothing more than to rip off her suit, take a deep breath of fresh air and lie down, but there wasn't any air, and more than two hundred people would die if she didn't find a way to communicate with the oko.

"You said you'd figure it out." Manolo's voice came though her speakers with a high-pitched clipping sound, an effect of the diluted gases added to their air supply.

"I meant it. Just give me some more time." It was Kahikahea's responsibility to see beyond the surface, to be the problem solver for the crew of the *Lamprey*, the outside-the-box thinker. They'd chosen her to save them, but the oko were just too alien. She couldn't figure them out.

"Two days. We won't be able to keep the scrubbers going after that," Manolo sighed, his voice a croak as he turned slowly away. "I'm going to recommend we disengage. Take our chances back in Einsteinian space-time."

"It's suicide." The chances of the *Lamprey* resolving into normal space anywhere near an Earth-like planet were too slim for even Kahikahea to calculate. "We'll be dead just as fast out there."

"What other choice do we have?"

Humans couldn't survive in the thin swirl of toxic gases filling the oko canyons. The *Lamprey* had exhausted its air supply weeks ago, its reserves days ago, and was now at the limit of its scrubbers. They needed to get home or get help. They needed the oko.

"I don't know." Kahikahea took a deep breath, instantly regretting the waste of good air. Manolo was right. She'd been their only chance, and she'd failed.

She'd tried every form of communication, from light, to sound, to smell, from symbols projected on a moving screen, to sending a probe skittering around the creature's heads like a nagging fly. Nothing. No contact – no *recognition* of any kind. Without communication, they were as good as dead.

"Let me try one more time," she pleaded, staring down the ridge to where the drone platform had crashed. "I'll pilot the platform myself."

A stripe of dark – so black it hurt the eyes – circled the chasm just below the ledge, a counterpoint to the riot of color above. Slashes of intense sapphire and lime crossed cherry-red bars along the walls of the upper chamber, confusing the senses, and leading Kahikahea to wonder if the oko were color blind.

One of the creatures had lurched into the canyon from the darkness of the next chamber. It shuffled slowly across the trough, blocking the original oko's path. They continued toward each other as if unaware they weren't alone, never slowing. Kahikahea winced as they made contact, expecting a thunderous boom as mountain met mountain, but the oko stopped just in time, their bodies seeming to melt together. Then, after a brief hesitation, they turned aside and continued along their original trajectories.

"That was weird," Manolo said.

"It was." Kahikahea had studied the creatures since her ship had piggybacked onto the oko vessel's hull over a month earlier. They were solitary, and it was rare to see more than one in a chamber at a time. "I wonder—"

The oko stopped. They rotated to face each other, and Kahikahea's nose started to bleed. Sharp-edged pain shot through her jaw. She staggered, and Manolo fell to his knees beside her.

"What was that?" he gasped.

"They *can* talk," Kahikahea said as the pain quickly subsided. She got the distinct impression there was meaning in that ultra-low frequency noise. "Just not to us."

"I know it's possible now," she said, slamming the last piece of the platform back into place. It looked like a curved shovel blade made from black lace, its basket an oval tub suspended below.

"They've never noticed before. What makes you think they'll notice now?" Manolo's face was a blur behind his visor. She couldn't read his expression, but the anxiety in his words told her enough.

"They'll notice because we *need* them to notice," she said. "They've got to bring us back to Earth, and soon."

Oko vessels had the ability to travel many orders above the speed of light, something beyond mankind's capacity. They were predictable, as oblivious to human presence as a dog was to a flea riding on its back, and that made them perfect for piggybacking rides.

Until the *Lamprey* attempted it.

The oko abandoned their route for the first time, stranding the *Lamprey*'s crew, and making first contact not only essential, but desperate.

"Get in," Kahikahea said.

"No. Why?" Manolo had his gauntlet on the edge of the basket. He pulled it away as if it were on fire.

"Yes. Now," she commanded. "I need you to pilot this thing while I think. We have to get it right this time."

Manolo reluctantly pulled himself into the basket and linked into the controls. The platform shook. It tilted precariously as it lifted off and soared toward the nearest oko.

"How close?"

"Put us in its path," Kahikahea said. Manolo grumbled, but complied.

The creature had started moving, seeming to fall towards them like an avalanche. Manolo jerked the platform. It skittered to the side, spinning.

Kahikahea grabbed his shoulder. "No, keep us in front."

"It'll crush us!"

"I don't think so." She remembered the way the two oko had touched before recognizing each other. Maybe that's what she'd been doing wrong. Maybe the oko needed contact to initiate communication. "But if I'm wrong..."

The oko filled her sky. Individual ripples in its flesh moved like tidal waves across its immense body as the creature loomed higher and higher, falling over them like a collapsing mountain. Kahikahea exhaled. She hadn't realized she'd been holding her breath.

Manolo choked back a noise, and Kahikahea whimpered, suddenly unsure. "It's not stopping."

She thrust out her hands as if she could halt the rumbling surface. Icy cold penetrated her gauntlets. She trembled, her heart nearly exploding as she felt the pressure of the oko's body touch hers.

Then it stilled.

The oko became as solid as stone. Kahikahea's gloves brushed its surface, and it felt wet, like week-old gelatin.

"I can't believe—"

The oko turned, its flesh sliding out from beneath her hands like iced-over snow, and it lumbered away.

"No!" She screamed in frustration. She'd been so sure. "That *had* to be it, just had to."

"It recognized you," Manolo said. "You got an oko to stop, and you didn't kill us in the process. That's a start, isn't it?"

"It's not enough—"

Kahikahea had been overconfident when they'd first realized they'd been stranded, thinking she'd be able to get through to the oko with little difficulty. She'd been trained in the basics of every imaginable subject, grounded in all the sciences and taught to look at any problem from as many angles as it took to solve that problem. She thought she knew everything. She'd even convinced the captain to follow her lead, but in doing so she'd used up valuable time and extinguished their remaining options. Her ego had killed them all.

Kahikahea's nose itched. A trickle of blood slithered over her lips.

Her teeth ached. A cold tingling raced up her spine, bringing with it a rush of adrenaline and the feeling that her head would explode. She clawed at her helmet. Her fingers fumbled the quick release tabs, frantic to get the noise out of her mind, desperate to make it end.

The hiss of escaping air stopped her. She gasped, dizziness threatening to topple her from the platform, hypoxia driving a wedge through her panic.

"They're speaking."

If they spoke, then they'd listen.

Kahikahea forced herself to concentrate, the pain ripping at her thoughts, disrupting her as she poured all her strength into a plea for help. The oko stopped. It swiveled back in their direction, its upper tentacles rushing by in long, whip-like arcs, each braided strand as wide as a three-lane highway.

"Help us! Take us home!" Her thoughts matched her screams as she collapsed, a warm trickle of blood covering her trembling lips.

Then, as quickly as it had started, the pain stopped, replaced by a very low voice in her mind. "We hear you now."

D. A. D'Amico writes beside a lighthouse on Plum Island in Newburyport, Massachusetts, USA, but the calm ocean breeze does nothing to quell the chaotic ravings in his fevered mind. He's a winner of L. Ron Hubbard's prestigious Writers of the Future award, volume XXVII, as well as the 2017 Write Well award.

New sci-fi podcast beams in from outer space

A new podcast from award-winning sci-fi magazine Shoreline of Infinity is launched, bringing the best fiction and news from around the galaxy.

Broadcasting from a satellite called Stella Conlator, Soundwave features audio dramas, interviews, music and poetry, all narrated and performed by brilliant voice actors.

"We believe in the thought provoking power of sci fi," explains host RJ Bayley. That's why we're inviting listeners to join our intergalactic Guild."

The first episode was released on the 1st of March 2019 and features Anne Charnock, JS Watts, Barry Charmon, Debbie Cannon, Sue Gyford and the music of Alex Storer.

Other great writers in series 1 include Richard A Clements, Catriona Butler & Rob Butler, and Matthew Castle, while The Infinitesimals will be creating and performing brilliant audiodramas.

Watch out for interviews with some stellar authors.

Soundwave will be released twice every month on the 1st and 15th and is available in all the usual podcasting places.

**for information and links to the podcast visit
www.shorelineofinfinity.com/soundwave**

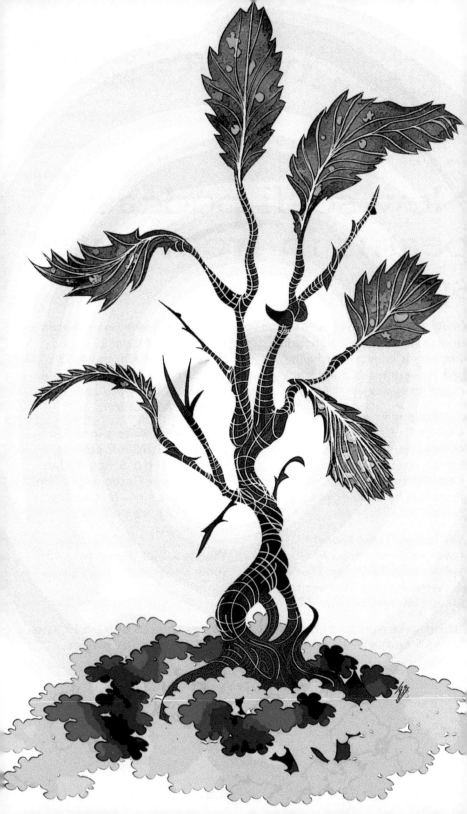

The Next of Us

John G. Sarmiento

The Next of Us might need enhanced spines. They'll carry a different weight, in a world more massive, cooler. It might have berries as unforgiving as a black mamba. Perhaps their stomachs should be enhanced as well. Humans who can eat poison. Imagine that.

Lyca and Sefo had argued and screamed at each other. Now the siblings quietly sat facing each other and sipped breakfast: steaming bowls of bulalo, hot moats of beef broth around scoops of rice.

"I'm sorry," Lyca said, "for throwing the bolt cutter in your vicinity."

"You almost didn't miss."

"I mean it."

"Accepted," Sefo pointed at the clock.

The siblings slurped their soup and ran out of the apartment, into the morning: a distant star burning and beaming in all directions.

"Remember," Lyca said over her shoulder, "soon as the bell rings."

"Let's manifest our imaginary friends. They love to migrate."

"We need all our faculties in the present."

"I have wings." Sefo ran ahead. "I soar!"

"Stay on the sidewalk. You don't have wings, and we only recently evolved to run."

During lunch, several students stayed cool in the library. They roamed the maze of books, running index fingers along jackets. Here and there a child picked a tome filled with drivable, flyable machines and creatures. These students didn't know how to sit and eat in circles. They didn't know how to tell stories eliciting laughter, spills, or stains. They knew only the shoes worn by their peers, but when Lyca entered the library, they all nodded.

Lyca pulled the bolt cutter out of her backpack and led Sefo through the aisles. They zigzagged to the back of the library, where they stood before the tallest door in the world. This door was padlocked.

"If it really makes you happy," Lyca chewed her lower lip, "then here." She offered Sefo the bolt cutter. "If we're caught—"

Sefo nodded. "Thanks!"

"Quiet. Wait for my signal."

"Signal?"

"I'll tap dance."

She scuttled down an aisle, glanced across a few rows, listened, and gave the signal.

Sefo cut the padlock, opened the door, and froze. When Lyca's hand squeezed his shoulder, he wasn't sure how much time had lapsed. "Lunch ends soon. Let's split up."

The siblings rummaged through the banned books. Gone were tomes with talking animals and children who lived with two parents. They heard soldiers, tanks, and planes blasting each other. Lyca traced miles of barbed wire, walls, and tents. Sefo stood over large pits of flies. Lyca ran from mushroom clouds. Sefo rode empty fishing boats and inhaled the dust over barren fields. Lyca saw glaciers and islands melting. Sefo felt bridges, churches, and libraries burn. The shrinking worlds were without trees.

"Trees, trees," the siblings repeated in whispered prayer.

"We have a few more minutes."

Even within these worlds they heard the bell ringing, telling them to march with the children.

After school they walked home side by side.

The apartment building surrounded a courtyard where the blue gazebo stood. In the gazebo's shade, the siblings' sapling grew. Its thin trunk was twisted, twisting. Its duct-taped branches begged for rain.

"Over-exposure."

"It's surrounded by a building," Lyca said.

"One day we'll build a tree house in it."

"Maybe the problem isn't the incision and grafting," Lyca suggested. "Maybe it's water quality, quantity." She slowly watered the sapling. "I filled this yesterday to let the chlorine evaporate."

She wondered where the blueprints of the building were, if water lines ran beneath the courtyard. She and Sefo could tap into one, redirect the water, and create a moat around the sapling.

"Soil quality, insects." Sefo pointed at a spider.

"Don't kill it. Biodiversity. Put it in the grass."

They noticed someone sitting, panting in the gazebo. The man glided towards them carrying two sticks. Lyca occasionally saw him twirling sticks and swords in the courtyard.

"You're from the third floor. Where's your mother?"

"You know our mother?" Sefo glared.

"Is she looking out for you?" Joel glanced at their apartment.

"She ensures our constant well-being."

"She's the first person we tell of our achievements." Lyca matched his gaze.

"She looked tired this morning. I wouldn't mess with her. She has two jobs?"

"We're her priority."

"I mean you no harm. Why are you out here?" Joel pointed at the tree. "That looks weird, sick, dead."

Lyca patted the soil. "It's alive. When we're successful, this will yield fifty kinds of fruits."

"Fifty," Sefo stressed. "But we have to be patient. Then we'll plant a circle of them around the gazebo."

"Why?"

"We used to grow our own food," their mother often said at the end of the month. Her voice echoed inside the refrigerator. "We made ourselves. We acted."

"To bend nature to our will," Lyca shrugged. "Proof of intelligence."

"Your mother taught you this?" Joel knelt and inspected the sapling.

"We taught ourselves."

"You're not afraid of me."

"There are scarier things in the world," Lyca replied.

"There are."

"You're Joel the swordsman." Sefo pointed at unit five's door.

Lyca scolded Sefo with her eyes. "We're going to kick the ball and run around."

"Will you turn pro someday?"

"We'll run around like kids do. We'll climb up and down everything, maybe perfect our cartwheel."

Joel fished a red object from his pocket. "You know what this is?"

"A whistle," Sefo replied.

"World's loudest. Take it."

Lyca nodded at Sefo.

"Put that on the nightstand. If you need help, if you're in danger, blow into it. I'll come running."

"We're supposed to call the police."

"A good neighbor's faster."

"Will you teach us how to use a sword?" Sefo grinned.

"Eskrima wasn't taught by monks. Be good."

"Was that a yes? I think he meant yes." Sefo raised his hands. "Wait, we don't have a nightstand."

"Don't put it in your mouth. Wash it first."

Sefo still held the whistle when he pulled the blanket over his chest.

"Did you floss?" In Lyca's mind, she already swept the floor. She was already washing dishes.

"I like the swordsman." Sefo yawned. "Maybe he's not dangerous."

"He practices. Go to sleep. We can't be late again." She peeked between the curtains, surveying the parking lot below: the darkest corner in the world. There the dumpsters waited. Lyca thought about the metal box under the bed.

Last year, her mother had sat on the bed and presented the box. "You two are always grabbing and climbing everything. I'm not surprised. You were grabbing my kidneys on your way out. Sit next to me. Listen, if you're in the kind of trouble you can't think through, if and only if, you can't sense a future, then run in here. Open this box. Pull this out. Take it off safety. Like this. Point this end, brace your arms and abs, and squeeze. See?

"Here. Stand up. Practice. Feel the weight. Point it at the wall. Higher. Aim below the chest. Aim small. Do you feel that? That's what screaming people feel. Some want to feel that way all the time. They have no self-control. You must recognize them. They're the worst of us. Worse than that thing you think lives just behind you. If they ever stand in front of you, go through them. You know what you'll become?"

"A hunter." Lyca shrugged. "A soldier."

"Proof I don't know what I'm doing, but I won't hear you screaming and begging in my head."

"We're not victims. We don't beg."

"And if you ever see a chased crowd, get ahead of it."

***

Sefo wiped his eyes with the blanket. "I thought about the future like you said. Drew my thoughts. You can see them if you want." He pointed at the floor. "Under my backpack."

"Right now?"

"Consider it. We can't watch trees grow. We can't perceive time like that."

"After I take the trash out."

"I can watch you from up here. I have the world's loudest whistle."

"You need good sleep without paranoia."

"Okay but leave the door open."

"Did you say your prayers?"

"I did not. And the curtains."

Lyca finished her chores to keep the dumpster rats from moving in. They were responsible for the bubonic plague. She picked up Sefo's notebook and walked into the kitchen, where three chairs leaned on the table. "Mars wasn't the answer," she read aloud to wake herself. The sentence startled her. Fatigue tugged at her eyes, but they darted across Sefo's jagged penmanship with curiosity. "When the world shrank, only one question mattered: Which planet?"

Scientists argued until they could imagine flying beyond the solar system, to walk on a specific planet's dirt, breathe the air, and bathe in the warm light of another sun. Before jungles and forests burned, before continents grew bald and dried, scientists agreed on a planet and a plan.

High above Earth, engineers built an antimatter engine and a ship, a microhabitat, around the engine. A trembling Earth shot this ship at a twinkle among twinkles, knowing the trip would take ten generations. The crew would become parents, and parents had to teach their kids. They had to teach their kids how to be scientists, engineers, pilots, farmers, chefs, doctors, and soldiers. Even if the moms and dads pulled double shifts, or double duties, even if the artificial day felt long, parents had to teach their kids how to live.

The tenth generation will land and walk on sand for the first time. They'll swim and gasp at their sunburned skin. They'll unload seeds and cultivate livestock DNA. Once sheep shuffled between trees and grass, the humans will assemble their most precious cargo: The Sefo Interplanetary Teleporter. Powered by the antimatter engine, the SIT will connect with its twin on Earth. The machines will fold the Milky Way between them.

Lyca scrutinized page after page of her brother's sketches: growing schematics for smaller and smaller segments of his teleporter, which looked like half of a massive bridge.

"Sefo, you awake?" He was having a hard time sleeping lately. After questioning the neighbors, Sefo had learned that a previous tenant had overdosed on opioids and drowned in their bathtub. Sefo kept seeing the man's ghost walking around the apartment, screaming at himself, at Sefo.

"I am not praying."

"No, I'll help you. I want to help you."

"Your clothes already become mine."

"I'll only help."

"Let's start tomorrow."

"We'll walk to the junkyard, start collecting parts, but does it have to be this big?"

"You need twice the size of that to travel dimensions, but the prototype could be smaller."

"Much smaller?"

"We won't be able to travel to another planet."

"Can we go anywhere else on this planet?"

"There might be life elsewhere."

"Are you thinking what I'm thinking?"

"The Library of Congress."

"The Library of Congress."

"Nice."

"What happens if the wormhole can't be contained?"

"Maybe nothing. Maybe it grows and consumes the whole universe. Probably nothing. What's for breakfast?"

"Leftovers."

Sefo groaned.

"You know what Mom always says."

"We have clean clothes and leftovers."

Beneath Lyca's feet, two people were yelling. The couple below, every night they argued. Every night they fought and shattered and glued together bits of their lives. Lyca crouched, crawled, and listened through the cold tiles. They always dressed like they went dancing on the mouth of a volcano, drawn there by fire. No, they weren't fighting now. Every night. How many babies have they made? Where are they? Who takes care of them?

Suddenly the loudest whistle in the world wailed, and Lyca answered the first question of being: you choose to act, to create or destroy, or do nothing.

JG Sarmiento was born in the Philippines and raised on spaceships, time travel, and superheroes. He holds an MA from the University of Guam, where he taught composition, literature, and rhetoric. He now pitches stories in parabolas from the Mile-High City. His work has landed in several publications.

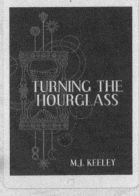

Spike

Lidia Molina Whyte

Nine pm pick-up was running late. Driver's fault, no doubt. Probably buggered his clearance or pissed off Border Control. Either that, or he was doing it on purpose. Nadia wouldn't be surprised. Cocky bastards thought they were better than everyone else just 'cause they breathed Safe air on drop-offs. "Cannae even lift half a crate anymore, pet," they bragged. Made a big show about it too, lifting shaky half-crates of faulty Gen while huffing and puffing, squinting their eyes like they just walked into the Dump without masks.

Load of pish.

Kyle used to be a driver before he got thrown in the pokey. He'd told Nadia all about the airlock systems, the sealing gas and the pigs ready to blow your head off if you so much as sneezed. Drivers could talk shite all they wanted but, in the end, they were just as ill as everyone else.

No point calling them out, though. If a shitebag driver had it in for you, a twenty-minute delay was the least of your problems. Best keep your head low, your mouth shut and your work going. And that's what Nadia did. She paced around the empty Warehouse, ignoring her shaky hands and taking stock again. Seventy-two empty bottles of Gen divided into six crates. Eight faulty. The rest to be refilled. The clock above the shutter door marked 9:24. Seventy-two empty bottles of Gen divided into six crates. Eight faulty. The rest to be refilled. 9:26. Seventy-two… Och, fuck it. Her throat was dry, she was covered in sweat and she couldn't even hold the clipboard straight anymore. Not even thinking about Maggie helped.

That's how she kent it was bad. And that's why she did it.

She let go of the clipboard, making it float in the air. The crates were next, lifting from their pallets and moving in circles without touching each other. Nadia made sure they were hidden by a shelf. If anyone clocked it, she'd be in shite so deep she might as well take herself to the Dump. Better than letting the medics in her head. 'Cause that's what they'd do. Smash her skull open to measure her Kem levels, or dunk her in some cryocoffin to study the K-Virus. Or worse. Make her… do things she didn't want to do.

Nobody would do that to her again.

Still, distracting her brain, focusing it on the clipboard and the crates dancing in the air, was the only way to stop the DTs.

"You'll give yerself a sore heid if you keep going on like that."

The clipboard slammed against the floor. Nadia caught herself before the crates did the same, putting them down gently before Jim clocked them too.

"Fuck, Jim. Scared the life outta me."

"Sorry, pal. Dinnae want you tiring yerself oot," he pointed at the load with his pen. "No' with all this to go."

Nadia buried her shaky hands in her pockets and smiled as if her heart wasn't about to punch through her chest.

"Doesnae look like I'll be lifting that anytime soon."

They both checked the clock. 9:38. Maggie would be raging by the time Nadia made it to The Steamy. She'd be banging on about joining the Union and fighting for Kins' rights all night. Nadia loved Maggie more than anything, but she didn't have the energy to change the world tonight. All she fancied was a pint and a laugh.

"What'd ye think's keeping this one?"

"Probably polishing his Daily Allowance with one of Lady Flavia's girls."

"Could be the new regs," Jim chewed the tip of his pen. "Heard folk are having trouble at the Old Town checkpoints. Something aboot a new spike batch. You ken anything aboot that?"

Nadia didn't, and she wanted to keep it that way.

The shutter door gave a loud bang. Thank fuck. Jim pressed the button and the door rolled up, letting the driver in. Something wasn't right. The lorry was too slow, too jumpy. It hadn't even gotten to the pick-up perimeter when the brakes squealed like a Dumper in the sun. The driver fell out while the lorry was still moving, unconscious and covered in blood.

Fraser is not the kind of man you fuck with. Not if you know what's good for you. The Kin fixing his Vertex must've missed the memo. It's the only excuse for his incompetence. Only in the fucking D Area would they let a Kin take over motor services.

"Look, *buddy*, I have somewhere to be. Can you pick up the pace?"

"Am very sorry, sir. Almost finished," comes the Kin's muffled response. His upper body is buried beneath the Vertex and Fraser fights the urge to burst the useless idiot's kneecaps.

It takes the Kin ten whole seconds to will a wrench from the toolbox into his hand and Fraser can almost hear his brain cells grunting from the effort. He lights a fag and contemplates spilling the Kin's bottle of Gen. In the end, he decides not to. Leaving the Kin without beer would be crueller than doing his legs in. Fraser's too much of a nice guy for that. Sometimes, he even feels sorry for Kins. Must be tough, drinking that stale piss day in, day out as if it were fucking ambrosia.

"I really need to get going," Fraser presses after he's finished his fag and the Kin still hasn't emerged from under the Vertex. He's really pushing it now.

To think they'd believed telekinesis was a gift, an *asset* after the war. As if lifting a couple of pounds or unwrapping a macrobiotic bar with your brain made you special. Fraser smirks. Didn't take them long to figure out it was just another side effect from the nuclear devastation, a fucking disease that rotted flesh and bone slowly, one breath at a time. Still, good to keep them subdued. Get them to drink their Gen like the good fucking boys and girls they are.

Lest they think they're something more than walking corpses.

This one won't be walking much longer. When the car creeper finally rolls out from under the Vertex, Fraser fights a wave of nausea. The Kin's skin is so yellowed and blotchy it reminds Fraser of a ripe blue cheese – the smell is just as bad, too.

"All done, sir. Leak was causing all sorts of trouble down there," the Kin explains, lifting himself up and grabbing the Gen in one fell swoop. Like all Kins, quick when it suits them. He takes a long swig and wipes his face with his muck-covered hand.

"Right," Fraser cuts in before the Kin launches on another apology. "Mr Novak is to take any future repairs from now on, got it?"

That shuts him up alright.

"Tell him my father, Mr Hills of Westminster Liquors, sends his regards."

Fraser loves to see that look on their faces. In the distillery, on the street, at Lady Flavia's... doesn't matter where. He lives for that sweet combination of fear and respect that makes even a Kin's bloodshot eyes beautiful.

"I will, sir." The Kin keeps his eyes on the floor and drinks his Gen. "Have a good night, sir."

The crisp smell of Italian leather greets Fraser when he finally slides into the driver's seat. His boot is the perfect match for the accelerator, and he spills onto the highway, crushing the toolbox on his way out. His phone beeps and he pulls the text up on the dashboard screen.

Granny's Green Steps. 11pm.

Fraser is going to have a good night indeed.

Fountainbridge was dead quiet when Nadia finally left the Warehouse. As soon as the pigs were out of sight, she kicked back her Daily Allowance in one big chug. Ah, that was better. Any other night, she'd be raging her Gen was warm 'cause of some glaikit driver. But not tonight. Tonight, it went down a treat.

It had been 429 days since Nadia had last spiked, but she remembered the feeling alright. A shot of pure, unfiltered joy. Like when you dig out a clean relic after a scavenging sesh down at the Dump or win The Steamy's death pool. Except you didn't have to break your back and nobody had to kick the bucket. Only thing came close to it was fucking Maggie. The stuff the driver was on must've been cut with some bad shite. Or no cut at all. In all her years using, Nadia had never seen anything like it. Bulging, veiny neck, spit gathering in the cracks around his lips and blood, a fuck load of it, pouring out of his eyes, nose and mouth, streaking down his chin and wetting his clothes. And the smell. A mix of the stale McKenny's Synth Burger he'd thrown up all over himself, piss and sweat that still clawed at Nadia's nostrils. It'd take weeks to get it, and the blood stains, off her overalls.

She needed another beer, and fast. She hurried down the street, glad to be distracted by the wall-turned-mural that ran all the way to Lothian Road. Someone had graffitied a naked lass popping out of a bottle of Gen. Nadia liked that one better than all the 'War is over but we're still dying' and 'Fuck the Healthies' sprayed everywhere else. Made her think of Maggie, except Maggie wouldn't get her tits out for beer. She only did that for just causes.

Unlike the streets, The Steamy was heaving. Nadia barely made it to the bar.

"How hot is it?" she asked Danielle, pointing at the week's death pool fund.

"Pretty hot after yer pal's donation," Danielle passed Nadia two pints of Gen. "Ballsy lad, that one, picking a Healthy. Especially after Maw Susie's physical."

Maw Susie, who was hunched in her usual spot at the bar, raised her pint.

"What pal?" Nadia dropped the change into the fund.

"Didnae catch his name. He's been buying Maggie drinks all night. Tall lad, handsome, tattooed neck... You OK, pet?"

No. It couldn't be. The drinks floated behind her as she shoved her way to the table where she'd first met Maggie, 429 days ago. *Their* table. Beer spilled on folk's heads, but everyone was too pished to care.

Kyle was sat on Nadia's seat, chatting to Maggie. Sweet, bonnie Maggie, who'd helped Nadia get clean, holding her tight every night when the DTs had been too strong to sleep. Who'd patched up all the cuts and bruises that Kyle had left behind, even the ones Nadia didn't wear on her skin. Who'd never said anything about how much Nadia could lift. And now Kyle had his long, thin arm round her, smiling that smile Nadia used to live for once, but had learned to fear soon enough.

The pints shattered all over the floor.

It takes longer than Fraser anticipated to get through the Victoria Street checkpoint. The medic on guard isn't so keen on letting him through, even after he shows her his Government exemption slip.

"There is a protocol for a reason, Mr Hills. The E Zone is especially unsafe for Priority Uncontaminated Citizens such as yourself. I simply cannot let you through to a Risk Zone without authorisation of a Government employee, who must be present during the…"

"I understand the rules," he offers, not letting his frustration show in his voice. "However, I'm sure we can come to an agreement if…"

"There are no exceptions, Mr Hills. Chances of contagion in this area are 69.34%, we must take every precaution to ensure the K-Virus remains contained."

Fraser wants to bury his fingers in her dark, curly hair and slam her skull against the desk. Repeatedly. But Father wouldn't be too thrilled if he found out Fraser had fucked up a medic fresh out of training, no matter how much the stupid bitch had it coming. Especially not after this morning's private meeting.

"Fraser," Father had sighed, lifting his head from the report he was reading long enough to give Fraser one of his steely looks, "what did I tell you about these… escapades?"

Fraser's suit had suddenly felt too tight, the office too small.

"That they must fucking stop until the press cools off," Fraser had forced out through gritted teeth when he couldn't take the crushing silence any longer.

"Exactly." Father had signed the report before moving onto another file from the pile on his desk. "We all like to have fun, son, but for once in your life could you at least try to behave like a man instead of a stupid fucking infant? That's a PR shitstorm not even I can pull you out of. Understood?"

Oh, Fraser understood alright. He understood that Becky from HR was a fucking grass. Shit like this is why Fraser loves himself a Kin whore. They always know their place, and that place is on their knees.

He swallows his anger – pity he doesn't have a shot of whisky to wash it down – and tries another angle.

"You know Westminster Liquors, don't you, lovely?" He takes his black card out of his wallet. "Owners of Generic Beer, Gold Scotch and Powell Gin. Biggest consumer goods company in the UK. We're also big into philanthropy. And cutting-edge science schemes. A few calls, and I could get you into the K-Virus Maximisation Programme, no questions asked."

She frowns, but Fraser catches the glint of hesitation in her pretty brown eyes before she blinks it away. He's read her all wrong. She's no A Area daddy's girl playing at doctors. She's a C Area bitch with a chip on her shoulder clawing her way up the ladder. The type who've had to suck so much dick to get their minuscule share of power, they won't risk it unless you can give them more. And Fraser can give her plenty.

"What do you say, lovely?" he leans in. "A smart girl like you could be running a team of medics in no time. All it takes is a call. Just one call."

He has her now. And even though she doesn't have the powdered skin, the smudgy eyes and strong perfume he prefers, he finds himself thinking of her naked as she stamps the exemption slip.

"Always been a clumsy one, our Nads."

Nads. That's all he had to say for Nadia to stop raging and start shitting herself. And he kent it. Oh, he kent it alright. He even patted her arm, smiling away as Danielle mopped up the mess.

"Come, sit down," his hand felt heavier than a dozen crates. "Maggie here was just telling me all about her job at the school."

Nadia felt sick. She slumped into a chair, trying not to greet. Maggie leaned in and squeezed her shoulder, "Finn was talking about raising funds for the Prolonged Education programme. You never told me you had a cousin in the C Area!"

He'd gone and got Maggie pished. Maggie never drank more than her Daily Allowance, and that was only for the DTs. Cleaner than a green medic, her Mags. But staying sober around Kyle was impossible. He was as good a pusher as he was a liar.

"You alright?" Maggie asked, sensing Nadia's discomfort even through the high.

"Grand." Nadia had to get her away from Kyle. It would cost her big, but she didn't care. She wouldn't let him hurt her. "Get us another round, won't ye? Hear cousin *Finn's* been doing all the buying. On ye go, it's OK," Nadia lied when Maggie didn't move. Finally, she went up to the bar. As soon as she couldn't hear, Nadia turned to Kyle.

"What the fuck are you doing here?"

"Hey, that's no way to speak to yer favourite cousin."

"Favourite cousin my arse. When did ye get out? Thought pigs weren't so keen on big-headed trappers."

Kyle had got it into his head that he was going to deal to the Healthies in their own house. The day he got caught with 50 shots of spike at the West End checkpoint was the happiest day in Nadia's life.

"Ended up cutting myself a sweet deal." His beer floated up to his mouth. "And here I am, back with my Nads at last."

He put his hand over hers.

"So you're a snitch." Nadia slapped his hand away.

"I'm a fucking businessman, that's what I am." The beer floated back down to the table. "And you're my business partner."

Maggie was back before Nadia could tell him to shove it.

"Lovely to meet you, Finn," she put a beer in front of Kyle without sitting down. "But I'm feeling a wee bit sick, I think Nadia and I should head on home now."

Kyle grabbed Maggie's arm and pulled her down on his lap. Nadia froze when she saw the needle. It was so wee, but there was no mistaking the drop of spike on its end. Maggie saw it too, and her eyes went wide with fear.

"Let go of her," Nadia warned.

"Not until you agree to help me." He ran his lips over Maggie's cheek. Maggie closed her eyes. Nadia thought that was worse than seeing the fear in them. "Unless yer girlfriend here wants to give this very special batch of spike a try? Gave some to an old pal this morning. Pretty chuffed with himself, he was."

He gave Nadia a wink.

"You ken him, Nads. Was picking up a load at the Warehouse tonight, actually."

It took all of Nadia's strength not to smash her pint into his face. That would only put Maggie in even more danger. If the driver wasn't dead, he was close. That needle couldn't go into Maggie's bloodstream.

"Fine, I'll help you. But I need to do something first."

The shaking has everything to do with excitement and nothing to do with withdrawals. Fraser is not hooked on that Kin-subduing shit, he just needs – no, 'needs' isn't the right word – he *likes* to take off the edge. That's all. He has to put up with the Board's shit, the press's badgering and Father's expectations, he deserves to have some fun.

He climbs Granny's Green steps, heart pumping like his Vertex's engine at 300mph. He's more than ready for some fun. When he reaches the top, he takes a moment to marvel at the views. The Dump claims the South, a big stretch of nuclear debris and disease. But it's the North Fraser focuses on. His eyes are drawn to the Hills Tower, a nanotube middle finger rising above the A Area cityscape. Beautiful. Not just because it'll be his one day – though that certainly has something to do with it – but because it is genuinely an architectural feat.

"You're late."

The dealer waits for him by the ruins of Edinburgh castle. He's not too shabby-looking, for a Kin. Especially one in his line of work. He doesn't flinch when Fraser approaches. Fraser doesn't like that, but the guy's supposed to have the best spike in town so he'll give it a pass, just this once.

"New Med at the checkpoint," Fraser lights a fag, ignoring his twitchy fingers.

"I thought you Healthies could get past that no trouble," he brings out his own fag and makes a gesture toward Fraser's lighter. He takes the lighter, leaving a sachet of spike in its place. Sleek. Despite the cocky comment, Fraser is impressed.

"Oh, I got past it alright," he remembers the medic's hesitant brown eyes and smiles.

They finish their fags in silence and all the while the spike burns in Fraser's pocket. By the time the Kin disappears into the castle ruins, it's all Fraser can do to crouch behind a rusty old bench to shoot up. He plucks out a needle from the sachet, just a little something to tide him over until he gets to Lady Flavia's. He rolls up his sleeve and brings the violet spark to his forearm. It dissolves into his bloodstream as soon as it touches his skin.

Ten seconds is all it takes for it to kick in. A shot of pure, unfiltered joy. Like when you smash a global sales meeting or take a new race car for a test ride. Except you didn't have to slave over reports and strategies and you got to keep the ride after. The only thing that came close to it was walking into a room full of Kins ready to do whatever the fuck he wanted.

He stands up and he's flying. His body soars towards the Hills Tower as he drinks in the colours that only exist when you've spiked. He's never felt so warm, so light, so free. His arms are wings, and he would've spread them had he not felt something wrap around his ankles. He looks down and finds thick black coils digging into his calves – ruining his brand new, custom-made suit – snaking up his thighs and burying under his shirt. They drag him back to the castle's ruins and he can barely make out the dealer's distorted face.

The last thing he hears before everything goes dark is a woman's voice.

"Nadia, please, don't do this."

Maggie was greeting but Nadia ignored her. Had no choice. The Healthy was built like a wrestlebot, and Nadia was supposed to get him to Kyle's car without a scratch. She could lift more than any Kin she'd ever met, true. But it had been a long fucking day and Kyle was holding a needle to Maggie's jugular, so she wasn't feeling too strong. Besides, she was used to lifting crates. Crates didn't have blood pumping through them or insides you had to be mindful not to turn into outsides. Nadia couldn't just hear the Healthy's heartbeat, she could feel it hammering inside her head.

"Shut up," Kyle dragged Maggie along. Nadia bit her tongue so hard she tasted blood. "Just over here."

They went down Old Fish Market Close, where Kyle's car and two lads dressed in black were waiting. Could be Dumpers, could be undercover pigs, Nadia couldn't tell. Didn't matter.

One of the lads opened the boot. "Put him in."

Nadia dropped the Healthy into the boot just as he started spewing. Her head hurt so much she was sure her skull had caved in.

Kyle pushed Maggie onto her knees, fingers digging into her neck. "Alright lads? Sorry about the delay, my man here wasnae on time. Sure you'll teach him all about punctuality later."

"Kyle," Nadia leaned on the boot. "Let go of her."

"The other one," said the lad who'd opened the boot.

Kyle turned to Nadia. His eyes made her think of the times before getting clean, before Maggie. The beatings. The spike. The lifting dares.

"Nads, you heard the man." He pointed to the car. "Get in."

"No!" Maggie tried to get up but Kyle dragged her back down by her hair.

Nadia wasn't surprised. Raging, yes. But surprised? Not a chance, not with Kyle. He'd done every bad thing anyone could do to her. This was nothing.

"You see, at first I felt awful for telling my friends here all about your extraordinary levels of Kem." He pulled Maggie's hair harder. "But when I heard you'd got yerself a girlfriend, I got over it pretty fast. Don't blame you, though. I couldnae resist this either."

"Get in the car. Now." The lad pointed a gun at Nadia.

"After this, go to Danielle," Nadia told Maggie, "she'll have something for you."

Nadia liked to think Maggie would use the death pool cash to get out of this shithole. The C Area's schools taught all the way up to sixteen. But, deep down, Nadia kent Maggie'd never do that. She loved a lost cause, her Maggie.

Maggie said something, but her voice was already melting into the air. Nadia lifted the two lads first. It was easy, even with a splitting headache. She found their heartbeats in no time.

"What the…?" The words died in Kyle's throat. As soon as the lads fell to the ground, Nadia turned on him.

She dug into him alright, peeling away his skin, his flesh, his bones, taking her time. His screams drowned her ears, moving, living things. She could feel herself fading as she did it, but she kept going. She had to.

She wanted to.

Fraser opens his eyes to light. At first, he thinks he's dead. That whole 'death is a release from pain' thing? Bullshit. Fraser feels like he's in a fucking blender. Every bone, every muscle is ripping into a million pieces. Then he blinks and a fluorescent lamp comes into focus. He tries to cover his eyes but he can't move his arms. They're handcuffed to the table in front of him. He looks down instead. His shirt is covered in blood and vomit.

The fuck? This is his favourite shirt. He'll have to have another one made as soon as he gets out this shithole.

"Stay calm, Mr Hills," that voice... he's heard that voice before. He looks up to find the medic who'd given him so much trouble at the checkpoint.

"What the fuck is going on?"

His mouth is dry, his head is throbbing. He's not just coming down, he's fucking crashing into the Earth's core. The medic turns to a tray where there are several syringes. He sets eyes on the needle and suddenly he remembers. That dealer set him up! Flashes of the night come back to him. A Kin crying. Another Kin, looking tired as shit, blood coming out of her nose. She must've been the dealer's little bitch because he kept ordering her around. What else? Fuck, his brain really isn't cooperating.

"Where am I?"

The medic ignores him, busy with her needles. Fraser hopes it's a penicillin shot, he needs one right now. Followed by a nice steam shower. He'll have to get round the handcuffs for that, but it shouldn't be too difficult once they realise who he is.

"You have been exposed to the K-Virus in extraordinary quantities, Mr Hills."

Exposed to... what the fuck was she talking... Wait. It was the Kin. That bitch had used her Kin to transport him, like he was a fucking crate. And then she'd killed that dealer! Oh yes, Fraser remembers now. He was glad to see that fucker go, just a shame he couldn't do it himself.

"Look," the light is too bright and Fraser's really uncomfortable, "can you just let me go? Whatever this is, it can wait until I've had a coffee."

"I'm afraid that won't be possible, Mr Hills."

All Fraser wants to do is rub his eyes. He pulls at the fucking cuffs but they're made of platinum and he ends up hurting his wrists.

"Let me go right now or I swear my father will…"

"Your father is outside." The medic smiles at him, she's fucking smiling! "Along with Doctor King, who will be assessing you for the K-Virus Maximisation Programme in a moment. Now if you can stay still for me, please."

Doctor King? Why was Father outside with him? And then it dawns on Fraser. That Kin whore spewed her K-Virus all over him and now they wanted to see the effects. They wanted to use him as a fucking lab Kin. Well, fuck that.

"You should experience some slight discomfort…"

"Fuck off."

"Now, now, Mr Hills." She stabs his forearm with the needle but her voice is sweet. "No need to talk like that."

"You can't do this!" He shouts as she leaves. "You can't do this to me! I'm the heir to Westminster Liquors! I own you! Let me go!"

But the medic leaves, locking the door behind her while he screams.

Lidia Molina Whyte is a half-Spanish, half-Scottish writer based in London. Her hobbies include reading and fighting the patriarchy. She achieves the latter mostly through writing and directing sci-fi, fantasy and horror pieces, with a couple of her abuela's Roma curses thrown in for good measure.
Follow her on twitter @LidiMolinaWhyte to see what she's up to.

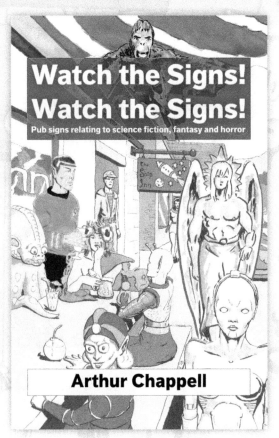

SCOTLAND'S FESTIVAL OF SCIENCE FICTION, FANTASY & HORROR WRITING

Competition for speculative short fiction - the results

The first Cymera/Shoreline of Infinity short speculative fiction competition was for previously unpublished writers living in Scotland.

We had two age categories: 14-17 year olds, and 18 years old and above. We were honoured to have two excellent judging teams who volunteered their time and their skills.

For the 14-17 group Laura Lam and Eris Young, and for the older group, Anne Charnock and Neil Williamson.

The two winning entries are published on the following pages, and each winner receives a prize of £75.

Without further ado, we announce the winners.

14-17 years Category

Winner:

The Woods by Cleo Luna

Runners-up

Life and Death by Simon Ezra-Jackson
The Creature by Daniel McConnachie

This is what the judges had to say about 15 year old Cleo Luna's story:

"Written in poetic, mature prose, The Woods manages to convey a great deal of vivid imagery for such a short piece of writing. With stream-of-consciousness narration the author builds a gradual portrait of a tragedy, shown in glimpses, as if through a covering of leaves."

18 years and above Category

Winner:

A Letter South by Beth Nuttall

Runners-up

Echo Chamber by Lyndsey Croal
The Weavers by S.A.M. Rundell

This is what the judges had to say

"We were impressed with the range of stories, enjoying everything from humour to horror, warnings to wonderment, glimpses of the magical and a variety of future Scotlands. An impressive display from rookie writers that promises well for the future of Scottish SF. While it was difficult to winkle out a winner, we felt A Letter South, with its quiet portrayal of a grim future, of an isolated community desperate to keep in touch with the outside world, offers a touching vision of a Scotland where there will always be hope."

Both Cymera Festival and Shoreline of Infinity offer our congratulations to the winners, a big thank you to our judges, and a massive round of applause to all our entrants.

The Woods
Cleo Luna

It's never been quite the same since the wood. Since we caught sight of the shiny dark tarmac, such a harsh contrast to the soft dryness of the sandy wood floor, since we laid eyes on others and left behind the trees.

It's not been quite the same. Nothing feels right, not the way people stare, or the way my skin flakes like brittle pine bark and that … that faint sort of ringing in your ears, that you can never quite figure out if it's real or just your brain playing tricks on you. Can you hear it? Just over the sound of your headache. Everything's slightly dull to the touch, quiet to the ear and bland on the tongue. Sand. Dust. There's nothing there but it's filling my mouth, clogging my lungs and caking my mouth.

I can see it in their eyes as well.

The others I stumbled out of the warm whispering woods with. Tom's. Even Ilana's. Their eyes are sort of… closed off. Closed-up, shut off and abandoned, their laughs blank. We all see it in each other's eyes. Branches and dappled sunlight.

Tom was the first to go. I wasn't surprised, the wood got to him first. Clouds floated through my head, snagging on twigs as I stared at his prone form, tall and pale like a fallen birch, dressed for nothing if not a cedar casket. The clouds muffled my ears as my eyes wandered up the vaulted ceiling in search of anything but brown, up the pillars and around the buttresses. We pride ourselves on individuality yet here is another testimony to our repetition: a church. Made of wood, shaped like trees, proof that we cannot escape our roots. The woods, again, present in everything. We were gathered to return another to the earth. Buried, back to the roots.

And then I looked down, in search of anything but branches, and I saw her. The dark oak benches reflected her cracked brown skin, her hair the curling, choking vines. Ilana sat on the other side of the coffin, eyes fixated on nothing at all and hands limp in her lap. Ah, I thought. She's gone too. Not in the same way though. Twists of sinew hardening into roots, feelings and thoughts cut short by waterless whispering. A hollow tree. Still standing but vacant. Lost.

Hushed tones echo and rebound. The wind brushing through autumn leaves. They mix and meld, an endless rushing whisper.

I smile.

And now I lie here, staring up at the blinding sun. Tom lies far to the left, drifting into the landscape. Ilana lies right beside me, but her pulse still goes strong. Not that she can hear it of course. She can't hear anything. So we lie together, the three of us, under the brown and blue.

There's a big oak tree above, the wind loud in its branches, rocking it from side to side. The corners of my mouth turn up, up, up to the blue sky and to the oak tree dressed in blue, and then I'm being pulled up by the oak, up, up, up to my roots and away. No, I think, no, I want Tom, and I look to him but he's not looking back, he's looking at the black of a body bag; and I look to Ilana but she does not return it. She's not looking at anyone, at anything anymore.

"Lost in the woods", the report stated. Lost? No. Not lost. Trapped, entangled and burned. Burned.

And now I'm staring at the brown branches in my white room, feeling the sharp needles in my soft pillows and I smile, because yes, it's never been the same since the wood but tell me, tell me, did we ever really leave the wood?

Cleo Luna is 15 years old. and lives in Edinburgh, Scotland. She has always loved reading in both Spanish and English, leading her to want to be a writer herself. She enjoys writing short stories in a variety of genres like sci-fi, fantasy, horror and adventure.

A Letter South

Beth Nuttall

Tigh Mor Beinn
Culnaglass
Coigach

12a West Heath Road
Broadmead
Hamps

26th April

Dear Megan,

Thanks so much for the photos you sent with your last letter!
The girls are getting big now – it's easy to forget how quickly
they change at that age, when I only hear them on the phone.
I don't have any photos as we still can't get hold of printer ink,
but I still take lots in the hope I can send you some eventually!

Spring has finally arrived here, the land has started to turn green and I'm writing this on the slope above the house. Behind me is the immense silence of the hills and in front the silence of the sea, and my hand has already started to go numb because actually, it's still cold.

The wind has dropped so I can hear water everywhere, and birds, and the whumph of the turbine in the distance. Along the road someone is herding their sheep and the boys are 'helping' turn over the veg garden with their usual shouting. But it's all just layers on top of the silence. Even the cars were like that. It would be easy to pretend that nothing has changed, from here. Gives me a dizzy feeling remembering all the times we were up here before.

Yes, it's all very idyllic today although it feels like spring has been a long time coming – maybe I'm getting old... Fortunately the house is pretty new and therefore well-insulated and draught-proof. The older cottages have mostly been abandoned now, or are being used as barns. There were still holiday homes being built here right up to the end, so folk have been able to move into them instead. Some of the more luxurious have hot tubs and so on, though as you can imagine it's quite hard to justify heating that much water :-)

There are still houses that are empty, too.

Sorry to hear about your bin situation – sounds horrible. I hope they've been cleared now, at least it wasn't too hot I guess. Would have been even worse in the middle of your summer heatwave. And I hope Dave has stopped being stressed about the electricity as it sounds like you're managing fine! I can't imagine why he is so desperate to keep his phone and tablet charged anyway since most of the time they're not connected to anything ;-) At least he's flying again now, even if he's getting most of his work from the military. You'd think they'd have the equipment to do their own aerial surveys...

The boys are both fine, in fact doing really well. Luckily for us they were young enough when we came here that they don't remember too much about the things they can no longer have. The teenagers and young adults are the worst – the ones that are left have a constant empty-handed look, as if they should be carrying something important. Actually, they are leaving here the same as they always did, looking for the future they should have had. The difference is that it no longer exists except inside their own heads. Hmm, maybe that's not so different really.

Anyway it's great for kids here: wandering unsupervised over the hills, catching hermit crabs in rockpools, flying kites on the big sand. So far we've managed to get hold of proper winter coats and hiking boots so they've been outside a lot right through the winters. I've lost count of how many old women have proudly informed me that the boys are having a 'proper' childhood, as if they are somehow responsible. And the boys are happy and healthy, and it's all good, but—

You asked if I felt sad about leaving Edinburgh. Not as it was when we left, that's for sure!

Mainly I regret not being able to give the boys the life I expected – all the things they could have done. Theatres, gigs, the madness of the Festival, cafe and restaurants, heated swimming pools with waves and flumes, football matches (though I'm quite relieved that I won't have to take them to any!). They won't even get to go to the cinema. I don't think staying in the city would have changed that. I mean, your cinema and swimming pool shut down, right? Didn't the cinema get bombed?

And coffee. You'd think I'd have got over it after this long.

Finlay's arm has fully healed now, thanks for asking. Luckily it didn't get infected although we do have a doctor here now and a pretty good stockpile of medicines. Seems like someone's still pushing hard to get them manufactured and distributed as they are easily available at the markets in Inverness. I'm so glad you found a supply of inhalers for Rebecca – fairly legitimate this time too, by the sound of it. I was really worried when you told me about being burgled, though I tried to hide it at the time. And the people who robbed you, how desperate must they have been to steal medicine out of a child's bedroom?

Another teacher arrived last month, which is great. She had cycled all the way from Dundee! She's good with the kids, gets on well with Mrs Malcolm. The two of them have some grand plans apparently, but for now they can divide the school between them and focus on a smaller age-range. The problem will come when the first child reaches high school age – at the moment Magnus is the oldest so a few years yet to work out how we can send them to the school in Ullapool. If it's still running by then. If there's any point in educating our children by then.

I've been working on some practical stuff, partly for the school but hopefully for everyone. There was a tiny library in the village hall here, used to be open only a few hours a week. Well, I've been expanding it. It's been very popular! Like you were saying there's barely any tv channels running except the news, so folk here have started reading! A triumph of the power of words etc etc. Or just boredom and a limited number of dvds...

The bookshops in Inverness are running out of stock but there are loads of places to pick up books for free – abandoned charity shops and so on – so I've tagged along on the last couple of trips and now we have enough to fill a whole extra room. Lucky electric cars have that extra space under the bonnet :-)

Everyone else here is either too busy or not interested enough in the endless sorting and running of the library though. It's a bit lonely wading through piles of books on my own. It would be good to have someone to work with.

Stewart and his dad have become totally obsessed with transport over the past few weeks. I know it's really important but if I have to listen to any more dinner-table discussions about how to build a path I think I will go mad! Occasionally they branch out into flights of fantasy about attaching solar panels to aeroplanes or something equally far-fetched, which is even worse...

Actually the path plan, although boring me to tears, is a good one. There's an old postie's path round the cliffs to Ullapool, much shorter than the road. Stewart and I walked it once and it was totally terrifying seeing the gulls wheeling below us while we stumbled and slipped along a 50cm notch in the rock. If we could make it safe for a bike and trailer however, it would mean a lot more people could get off the peninsula a lot more easily.

It would take a stupendous amount of work of course, but there seems to be plenty of volunteers. The folk who lived here before feel trapped without their cars, I think, even though they chose to stay because the isolation makes us safe. We haven't even seen any warships coming up the loch for almost a year. The ferry turned up last week though – who knows where they got hold of diesel! It was full of people leaving the outer islands. Must be hard there after this long. At least we can get hold of stuff from further inland when it's available, but nothing is going across the Minch now.

At the other end of the scale, Stewart and Alex – well, the whole committee really – are desperate to get hold of a plane and a pilot. A small plane could land on the straight, flat part of the road apparently. I can see how being able to fly over the mountains would solve many problems, but I can't imagine how any plane would get off the ground again once it was here with an empty fuel tank.

In the end though, I don't really care what happens to a plane once it gets here, as long as it gets here with you on board. What do you say? I know Dave continues to be loyal to his company but we both know it's only a matter of time before even their little planes are requisitioned. Nobody would come this far after you. How could they get the plane back down south from here?

I've had enough of worrying about you all, enough of being scared that every phone call and letter is the last.

There's space to live here, space and peace. I miss you. I want my nieces to grow up here with us. I want them to grow up.

All my love,
Stella

Beth Nuttal grew up in northern England, but settled in Scotland a long time ago. She lives in Cramond, Edinburgh, with her husband and two boys. Despite talking about books for 16 years with the Edinburgh SF Book Group, this is the first time she has tried writing a story herself.

The **BEACHCOMBER** presents ...

GREETINGS, EARTHLINGS! YOU KNOW THINGS **ON THE SHORELINE** ARE NOT **ALWAYS** WHAT THEY SEEM ...

STORY AND ART **MARK TONER** LETTERING **BLAMBOT**

COOEEE! MR **BEACHCOMBER**!

WHAT?!

IT'S **JOE AND TRIXIE** FROM **EARTH** -- YOUR **BIGGEST FANS**!

TOURISTS

HUMANS -- BUT IT'S **NOT SAFE** FOR YOU HERE!

WE'LL BE **FINE**. WE'VE BEEN TO **LOADS** OF EXOTIC PLACES.

THE **SHORELINE OF INFINITY** IS AN **ILLUSION** TO ALLOW YOU HUMANS TO COMPREHEND **SOME** OF WHAT HAPPENS HERE **WITHOUT** RISKING YOUR **SANITY**...
-- **BUT** IT IS A PLACE **ONLY SAFE** FOR **PANDIMENSIONAL** BEINGS SUCH AS **MYSELF**.

OMIGOODNIS!

NOW IT'S **TIME** FOR **YOU** AND **TRIXIE** TO **GO HOME**, JOE.

HAVE A **GOOD SUMMER** --

-- BUT **BE CAREFUL!**

Lost Part 2:
The Blue Country

Ruth EJ Booth

"Every day, the light brought the promise of something just beyond the mountains, the unexplored landscape. That glow fascinated me. I'd wanted to visit Svalbard for decades. I never imagined that, once I was there, I'd long for what lay beyond that horizon…"

Even in the depths of the polar night, you can find yourself a little light. This January, I found myself in Svalbard, speaking at an interdisciplinary conference on Darkness. At the nadir of the arctic winter, the town was swathed in darkness for the most part, though, once a day, a twilight glow cradled the peaks of the valley. I had come feeling, frankly, a little lost, but for those brief hours I caught a glimpse of comfort. In that rich glow, I imagined further North, the true North Pole. The undiscovered country beyond.

And it was a glorious lie. North couldn't have been in that direction. That glow was the ghost of sunrise, a light that could only have come from south of the islands. Sure enough, when I checked my map of Svalbard, the head of the Advent valley points south-west, or thereabouts. While I'd longed for the land beyond its walls, if I had followed that glow, I'd have found myself going back the way I came.

Last issue, I spoke of the relish with which we make writing resolutions. We like to imagine ourselves better, as our idealized selves, people who are only one regularly-attended, diligently-studied class away. And why shouldn't we? But, as anyone with a gym membership unused since January knows, hitting your targets is never straightforward. Aside from the difficulty of making and sticking to realistic goals, there is keeping your goal – your 'mountain', to use Neil Gaiman's terminology – in sight and working out which way to go[1]. There can be benefits to getting stuck on the path, though, allowing you time to take stock, consider your options and prepare, before carefully choosing your next steps.

Yet, we often forget that what happens on the journey might affect how we view our goals and aspirations. After potentially years of struggle to reach them, we might find that our mountains don't hold the same allure close up that they had from a distance. We may have to abandon long-cherished goals, never quite reaching the mountains we wished to climb. Rather than stuck, we may feel stranded: all our efforts for nothing.

Hunter S. Thompson's career was, in essence, a failure. He had aimed to write a novel about the death of the American Dream, that aspirational ideal of equal opportunity for all.[2] It's not that his success as a journalist and author meant nothing to him – far from it: Thompson had a cushy number in speaking tours, as well as the means to keep writing and living his legendarily hedonistic way well into his sixties; but the goal of producing this book was always on his mind – as well as his publisher's. Thompson never completed his magnum opus.

With this in mind, we might wonder why we bother having writerly aspirations. If a lauded genius like Thompson didn't reach his goals, what hope do we have? History is replete such examples – the theory of everything that eluded Stephen Hawking, for one. Would Thompson have been better off focussing on his journalism, rather than his albatross of a book? Would Hawking have been happier forgetting M-theory and sticking to black holes? Are we fooling ourselves in wanting to write that epic series when we might save ourselves the anguish of never living up to those expectations?

Rebecca Solnit's essay collection *A Field Guide to Getting Lost* contains not one, but two essays with the title 'The Blue of Distance'.[3] In them, she explores what she calls The Blue Country, the far hills we see on a clear day, that landskein of blues and greys stretching into the distance. This she considers a metaphor for desire, for, as alluring as those hills are, we never truly reach that blue space; by the time we do, they have changed colour, concentrated out of distant blues into greens and yellows, become concrete. Perhaps the value in those far-off places, argues Solnit, lies in more than just their status as a place to be reached.

Solnit notes how we only see desire as an itch to be scratched, rather than its inherent worth in providing us something to hope for, to value, an aim. With these desires, we structure our lives. But what if the value of what we aim at lies not in those things, but in the journey they inspire us to take?

Hunter S. Thompson never did write his book on the American Dream. In the end, the closest he got was several acclaimed features on the politics and culture of the US – two bestselling, critically acclaimed books – and becoming the figurehead of Gonzo Journalism, the movement that not only revolutionized non-fiction, but became a staple citation for every young buck wanting to piss his mark all over the world.

But if you look at Thompson's work, you'll see the American Dream lies at the heart of everything he did. It was that which drove him to crawl beneath the filthy underbelly of US culture, bring up the scrapings and, with the aid of some greatly underappreciated editors, sift them through for gems of narrative.

What seem to us like the pinnacles of a glittering career were just points on the way for Thompson. Without that greater goal of the American Dream, would he have taken the mescal-fuelled trip to the Mint 400 desert race that inspired *Fear and Loathing in Las Vegas* (1971)? Would he have followed Nixon on his '72 presidential jaunt for *Fear and Loathing on the Campaign Trail* (1973)? Rather than a failure that dogged his career, we might instead see Thompson's American Dream as a North Star, a blue dawn, leading him through and beyond things that, in hindsight, look to us like worthy enough goals on their own.

The stories we write to train ourselves up. The essays we tear up, and rewrite again and again. Maybe we won't reach the lofty goals we set ourselves: we might be looking in completely the wrong direction. But the steps they inspire us to take may lead to achievements just as worthy as those we originally aimed for. Perhaps even more so.

Upon his death, Hunter S. Thompson's ashes were loaded up into a rocket to be fired into space, watched by a crowd of well-wishers as they zoomed up into the stratosphere. But the rocket didn't make it that far. The ashes fluttered down through the sky to land on his guests, covering their clothes, hair, ruining their drinks: a move Thompson's long-time biographer William McKeen couldn't help but think was contrived that way.[4] Even if your mountain doesn't end up your final destination, you can still have a hell of a time on the way.

Endnotes

[1] For more on this metaphor and Neil Gaiman's guidance on writing careers, see Part One of this column, 'Further North', in issue 14 of *Shoreline of Infinity*.

[2] For an insightful biography of Hunter S. Thompson by an author who knew him, see William McKeen's *Outlaw Journalist: The Life & Times of Hunter S. Thompson* (London: Aurum Press, 2009).

[3] Rebecca Solnit, A Field Guide to Getting Lost (Edinburgh: Canongate, 2006), 27-41, 63-83.

[4] McKeen, *Ibid.*, 365.

Ruth EJ Booth is an award-winning writer, editor, and academic based in Glasgow, Scotland. For stories and more, see www.ruthbooth.com.

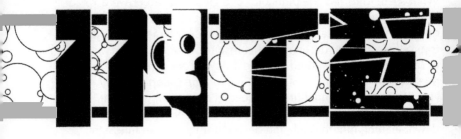

Louise Welsh – A Lovely Way to Talk

Iain Maloney talks crime, the apocalypse and crossing genres with the Glasgow based author, playwright and librettist.

Louise Welsh *is the author of 8 novels, short stories, plays and,
with Stuart MacRae, the opera* Anthropocene. *In* The Plague
Trilogy – A Lovely Way to Burn, Death is a Welcome Guest *and*
No Dominion – *a pandemic colloquially known as 'the sweats'
decimates the British population, bringing society to its knees and
ushering in an era of survival at all costs. The main characters,
Stevie and Magnus, flee from the crumbling civilisation for the
remote safety of Orkney before events draw them back into the
fray. A full review of the series was published in* Shoreline of
Infinity 14. **This interview contains mild spoilers.**

Iain Maloney: The first
thing I wanted to ask was why
science fiction? Or, perhaps I
should ask, do you think of it as
science fiction?

Louise Welsh: I think of it
more as speculative, something
that crosses genres. Although
I'm never sure that writers are
the best people to decide what
genre we're in. The publishers
asked me for a crime trilogy
and I think what I did was cross
genre – speculative fiction,

apocalyptic fiction with a crime
aspect to it. It's definitely got
the crime as part of the motor.

IM: What motivated you to
head in that direction, to take
the request for a crime trilogy
and head off at a 90 degree
angle?

LW: You've got to do what
you've got to do, haven't you?
You've got to tell the stories
that are in you and that story
was there, in me. I think these

things come from what you've read, the books that have influenced you. For me it was a childhood brought up in Scotland where you were sure the bomb was going to land on you at any minute. I love John Wyndham, *War of the Worlds, Death of Grass, Threats,* the 1970s series *Survivors,* that kind of apocalyptic fiction that is based very much in the world that we inhabit; it's not a glossy world, it's a world we recognise. But ultimately I think the story dictated the genre rather than thinking I'd like to write within that genre. It's more that the genre is where the story would fit.

IM: It's interesting that you mentioned John Wyndham there because when I was reading it I felt it was very much in that speculative vein: real people in real situations and then one fundamental thing changes.

LW: I love his books and yet when you go back and reread them they're quite... they're not comfortable, are they? They're quite racist, they're quite sexist, they're quite othering in terms of class as well. I think that's the other thing about a lot of speculative fiction of that era – it's often about what are people *really* afraid of? In the Wyndham books, or *War of the Worlds* – in *Death of Grass* especially – what are people

afraid of? They're often afraid of the working class and the removal of constraints, that the working class will descend into beasts, into the animals that they are. Whenever you're writing within a set genre, you're kind of having a conversation with those books as well. Because those aren't my feelings – I don't feel that the working class are only held in place by the structures of civilisation. So that was interesting to engage with as well.

IM: He's very much of his time – all speculative fiction is – and it hasn't all aged well. But his storytelling still stands up.

LW: Yeah, his storytelling is amazing. And it's also part of the interest that these books hold, because the reflect on the period and they tell us something about the period that straightforward histories don't. They give us the attitude and the voice of those eras.

IM: You described the trilogy as a crossover, that there's the crime in there as well as the speculative and apocalyptic. *A Lovely Way to Burn* definitely has one foot in the crime genre – it has a crime plot in a speculative setting – but by *No Dominion* the crime element has pretty much gone and it's straight dystopian/post-apocalyptic...

LW: It's *all* crime by that point! No, that's true, and maybe that's reflective of the breakdown in the society, that the crime aspect would take a different manifestation. At the beginning I was thinking about Big Phrama and what does Big Phrama do, but you're right, by the end the book is thinking about 'what kind of society do we want to live in'. You're right, there's not a straightforward villain, there's not a straightforward crime plot, it's more of a quest.

IM: I was curious while reading it, was there any conscious decision to start off with the crime aspect front and centre before dialling up the speculative elements? You've got a readership you've built up over a number of books who know you predominantly as a crime writer – at least that's how you're often marketed – so was there a deliberate idea to slide into a new genre this way to bring your readership with you?

LW: No, not at all. I am perceived as a crime writer but all of my books sit unsteadily within the genre. They never quite slotted in evenly, although I'm really happy to be regarded as a crime writer. You just have to go with where the story leads you and hope that people enjoy

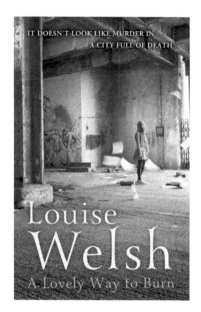

that journey and that story.

IM: How did the publisher react when you sent in the first one, which wasn't the start of the crime trilogy they were expecting?

LW: They were fine with it. They just marketed it like a crime novel! There was enough crime in it – at heart it's about justice and injustice, and in the first novel there's a straightforward murder plot – the first two books have murders in them and the third book has a different kind of crime, an apparent kidnapping. I'm saying I don't fit easily within the crime genre, but I do always have somebody getting killed! I'm not sure why that is.

IM: In the first book it's very much *there's been a murder* and Stevie's going to find out who did it whereas in *No Dominion,* there is a murder – the murder of the foster parents – but by that book there's so much death and destruction going on everywhere that another murder is lost in the background. By then the kidnapping seems much more shocking.

LW: That's part of the question people have to ask in war zones and places where everything is going to shit in that way, when there are so many deaths: does another death matter? And within the crime novel the answer is yes. The individual death does and should matter. But that level of death and destruction… it was a difficult canvas to work on. When you come to write those moments you pull the camera in real close on that particular moment to say 'look, it is still a person.'

IM: It's interesting you say that about the canvas: within the dystopian/post-apocalyptic genre, most writers dodge that. They either write up to the 'event', the moment of apocalypse, or they start their story in the aftermath amongst people who have no idea what happened. But you take us right through the heart of it and out the other side. Why did you decide to tackle it head on?

LW: I guess I just have a linear mind! I was very influenced by the 1970s TV show *Survivors*. As a child I liked to stay up late and watch that, and they began with this pandemic, they began with just a few characters and I think that really influenced me. But in the beginning I was thinking more about capitalism and I wanted to start in the heart of a great world city – I chose London – where there's this terrible contrast between the rich and the poor: who can survive and who can't. Just the rapaciousness of capitalism. But also the brilliance of that city where everything is happening – if you can access it, it's an amazing place. I wanted to start off with the image of this brilliant, cruel city. It's often the case that these stories about the end of civilisation are often a love-letter to the civilisation. We have this amazing civilisation that we are in, but it's a shame it's not a kinder place. There's a lot that we stand to lose and do we really want to lose that through casual, greedy over-reaching. But the history of humankind is always over-reaching. We always blow it in the end.

IM: Is that why you made Stevie work for a shopping channel?

LW: Yeah. I've always been

> **"It's often the case that these stories about the end of civilisation are often a love-letter to the civilisation."**

interested in that world, in sales. My dad was a salesman and I always found salespeople really interesting. I think the skills that you need to be able to sell stuff are similar to what makes you entertaining or fun to be with, so I kind of like the idea that her ability to sell is also what helps her survive. The skills that make her a good operator within capitalism help her survive afterwards. She's a survivor.

IM: It's a nice balance because in *No Dominion*, Magnus is the classic survivor: he's angry, he's drinking a lot, he's violent and withdrawn. He's how you expect someone in that situation to be, whereas Stevie is so different – just as logical but a different spin, that her skill set developed under capitalism allows her, in a sense, to thrive post-apocalypse. How much of the trilogy did you have planned out in advance?

LW: The overall arc, the physical journeys were all planned... the details weren't so planned. The most difficult thing was the ending because I had a more optimistic ending in mind but over the five years that I was writing these books the world changed. The world took some crazy turns. It's difficult – it's difficult for us as human beings but also for us as writers, to write fiction in a world where you have Trump, the stupidity of Brexit, we've got all these strange things happening. When I started President Obama was in the White House and when I finished Trump had just got in. So I guess that idea of things being more cyclical developed and that affected the structure of the final book and the outcome. You respond to the things going on around you.

IM: I think it's really interesting that you knew from the start that it was a trilogy because in many ways it's an unconventional trilogy. Stevie is the main character in book one but she's completely absent in book two and only returns in book three. While I was reading them I assumed you'd written *A Lovely Way to Burn* as a stand-alone novel, decided to write another book in the same universe – *Death is a Welcome Guest* – and then afterwards thought "Hey! I can tie these together!" But it sounds like you knew from the start that we'd lose sight of Stevie for a while.

LW: I'd always planned it that way, to shift from Stevie to Magnus and then bring them together. I wanted to start off with Big Pharma but I also wanted to look at what happens if you're incarcerated when something like this occurs, so I wanted overlapping timelines. I wanted a different point of view... I guess it's a very loose trilogy in a way. It's more the world and the circumstance that links them... it is a strange way to do it but that was always my plan, to do the trilogy like this and then stop and not do anything else in that world. And I'm going to stick to that although I really enjoyed being in that world – it took about five years which is a considerable chunk of your life so there was something quite tempting about staying in it.

IM: It's such a deep, rich world and I'd be very happy if you returned to it in the future. So much of the trilogy is them travelling through Scotland and there are all these other stories going on, so many paths you could go down.

LW: I can understand – you know when Michel Faber did *The Crimson Petal and the White* and then he came back and did a collection of short stories using the same characters – I could really understand how you might be tempted to do that after living in that world, and making it in your head and having so much left over – because there's always stuff left over – but I'm not going to do anything like that. It was fun to do but you need to move on to something else, to stretch different muscles and try different skills. You have to write the book you need to write because who knows how many books we have.

IM: Great Louise, thanks for talking to *Shoreline of Infinity*.

Iain Maloney is the author of three novels and a collection of poetry. His memoir on life in Japan, *The Only Gaijin in the Village* will be published by Polygon in spring 2020. www.iainmaloney.com @iainmaloney

About Writing – A Field Guide for Aspiring Authors

Gareth L Powell

Gareth Powell recently won his second BSFA award for his novel Embers of War. *He has also just released* About Writing – A Field Guide for Aspiring Authors: *the title tells you all you need to know. Gareth and his publisher, Luna Press Publishing, kindly allowed* Shoreline of Infinity *to include the introduction to his book in this issue.*

Gareth is appearing at Cymera 2019 — Scotland's first Festival of Science Fiction, Fantasy and Horror Writing.

I have a friend I want to tell you about, because the chances are you might know someone just like him. You might even be someone just like him.

Now, I don't want to embarrass my friend, so for the purposes of this book, let's call him Bill. I see Bill maybe once a month at various literary events, and sometimes in the pub. Bill wants to be a novelist. He really, really wants to be one. And not just any novelist. No, Bill has convinced himself that he's going to write one of the great books of our time. After all, he spends all his time reading and criticising other books. He's seen just about every film made in the past thirty years, and he has an opinion on just about any writing-related subject you care to mention.

Gareth L Powell (photo:TomShot Photography)

However, Bill never writes anything. Oh, he talks a good game. He's half-convinced everyone he knows that he's a serious author. He can tell you all about the book he's going to write. Like the character of Katin in Samuel Delany's novel Nova, he can rattle off half a dozen literary theories without pausing to draw breath, and without ever committing anything to paper. He never writes anything down for anyone else to read. Bill's convinced he has it in him to be a world-class novelist, but he's pushing fifty, working in a job he hates, and taking no active steps to achieve his dream.

Why?

Because Bill's expectations are too high. He's set his sights on writing a perfect novel without putting in the groundwork. He has so much of his self-image tied up in this idea of himself as a frustrated writer, a great talent waiting to be discovered, that if he ever actually finishes writing anything, and it isn't the shining masterpiece he sees himself as capable of producing, he'll be crushed.

So instead of writing, he makes excuses. He says he needs to find a physicist to check whether the physics of his idea are feasible; he says he needs to locate some obscure out-of-print book on sixteenth-century witchcraft; and he says he can't possibly work unless he's alone with his muse for a month in a cottage on the edge of Dartmoor. These excuses are his security blanket. They are obstacles he puts in his own way, to avoid having to confront the fact that writing novels is hard, time-consuming work, and the only way to do it is to sit down and start typing. Better to feel that he could produce a brilliant book if only he could afford to take a month off work, than to just get on with it and be disappointed by the results. Better to cling to the comforting notion that he's an unrecognised genius than risk disappointing himself by failing to live up to all his talk.

Earlier, I used the phrase "without ever committing anything to paper", and that's the key: commitment. I like Bill as a person, and I think the ideas he has are terrific, and I wish he would write them instead of talking about them. But he never does. Like the overweight middle-aged guy who still dreams of being a professional footballer but never trains or tries out for a local team, Bill lacks the commitment to put in the hard work needed to achieve his goal.

> "I will give you the best piece of advice I was ever given: just write the fucking thing."

If you want to write, you have to accept that the first draft you write will look pretty ragged. It will not be perfect. But the important thing is to get it written. That's the hard part. Once you actually have it all written down, it becomes real. It exists, and you can then take steps to polish and improve it. Expecting every word that flows from your fingers to be perfect first time is unrealistic and self-defeating, as you tend to get hung up endlessly trying to write the perfect first line, rather than ploughing ahead and telling the story.

I've spoken to a lot of writers who've told me that the first line, and sometimes even the whole first chapter, gets rewritten once the rest of the book is finished. So why waste your time trying to make it perfect, when the end of your book might suggest a different way for the story to open?

A couple of years ago, I wrote the following in reply to a question on my website, and I think the words are just as applicable to Bill (and all the other Bills out there). I wrote:

"I will give you the best piece of advice I was ever given: just write the fucking thing. Getting the words down on paper is the hard part. And it doesn't matter if your first draft sucks. All first drafts suck. The important part is that you write the story. Then, when you've finished it, you can go back and edit it, polish up the text to make it shine. Editing is easier than writing. So, if you have a story to tell, just write it down without worrying how it sounds.

You will not hit perfection first time. But you will get a completed first draft that you can then work on, to bring it up to professional quality. A lot of people make the mistake of trying to edit as they go along – of trying to make each sentence perfect before moving on to the next – and that is deadly. Just write. Tidy up later. Go for it."

And that's where this book comes in. I've been a professional writer for over a decade now; I've written ten novels and two collections of short stories, and I've learned a thing or two along the way.

There are a million books out there that will tell you about grammar and the importance of ditching adjectives. This isn't one of them. The pieces between these covers are despatches sent from the front lines: hard-won lessons from the last ten years. Things I wish someone had told me before I set out, and insights I've gleaned along the way.

I hope you find them helpful.

Especially you, Bill.

About Writing – A Field Guide for Aspiring Authors is published by Luna Press Publishing, £8.99, available from:

www.lunapresspublishing.com/product-page/about-writing

THE **SHORELINE OF INFINITY** IS AN **ILLUSION** TO ALLOW YOU HUMANS TO COMPREHEND **SOME** OF WHAT HAPPENS HERE **WITHOUT** RISKING YOUR **SANITY**...

Reality is a problem here at Shoreline of Infinity. This year we're looking for short tales which tweak reality. Your story could be set in the past, present or future, here on Earth, out there in space. Your story will bend your readers' minds, question their own perceptions. Scary, questioning, humourous, we don't mind – it's your reality after all.

Prizes:

£50 for the winning story plus 1 year digital subscription to *Shoreline of Infinity*. Two runners-up will receive 1 year digital subscription to Shoreline of Infinity.

The top three stories will be published in *Shoreline of Infinity* –All three finalists will receive a print copy of this edition.

The Detail

Maximum 1,000 words.

Maximum 2 stories per submitter.

The story must not be previously published.

Deadline for entries: midnight (UK time) 15th September 2019.

To enter, visit the website at:

www.shorelineofinfinity.com/2019ffc

There's no entry fee, but on the submission entry form you will be asked for a certain word from issue 15 of *Shoreline of Infinity*, hence: competition for Shoreline of Infinity Readers.

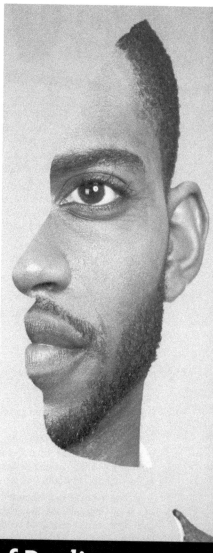

A Twist of Reality

Flash Fiction Competition for
Shoreline of Infinity Readers

REVIEWS

With the Cymera Festival just around the corner, we've taken the opportunity to explore hybrid works of science fiction. From science fantasy to genre mashing with horror or romance, we've got a selection that opens up our expectations of science fiction.

This is a time to really delve into all the layers of what a story could mean – and maybe teach us how to build a bridge of two? As always, we hope you enjoy our take on these wildly different tales and look forward to seeing you in the summer!

—*Sam Dolan, Reviews Editor.*

Tentacle
Rita Indiana, trans. Achy Obejas
And Other Stories
160 pages
Review by Eris Young

It's the mid-2020's, and a series of ecological disasters have left the seas around the once lush Dominican Republic barren, devoid of all life. Two very different characters are plunged into this mix of environmental and political turmoil, a world of Yoruba deities and art school dropouts.

Acilde is a maid in the house of a seer, Omicunlé, soothsayer to presidents and venerator of Yemayá, mother of the sea. Acilde wants many things but the foremost of these is Rainbow Brite: a black market drug that promises the user an instant, complete sex change. Argenis is an embittered ex-painter, caustic and bigoted. Lured by the prospect of money and the recognition he craves, Argenis joins a community of artists in a cliff house by the sea. But there is a deeper purpose to the artists' project, and the curator is not who he seems. From these two vastly different perspectives, we see plot and prophecy unfold across centuries, a desperate last attempt to save the ocean from contamination. Will it be enough?

A genre – and gender – bending tale of time travel and murder, *Tentacle*, (originally published in Spanish as *La Mucama de Omicunlé*) interrogates everything from contemporary art to gender politics. Told in a raw, tense, noir-like prose, and set against a crumbling Caribbean backdrop, this is an unflinching, lurid sci-fi epic.

Tentacle is gritty, delving deep into poverty, prostitution and government corruption, but it romanticises nothing and never descends into melodrama. Each and every one of the characters are flawed in some essential way – powered by greed, fear, self-preservation, religious fervour – sometimes to the point of unlikeability, and this is what makes them compelling. The author presents her characters, uncoddled and without comment; they are merely players in a larger drama as it unfolds, people fighting against fate, carried along in an unrelenting tide of events. When I read *Tentacle*, I got a strong sense of each character's offscreen experiences having shaped them, for better or worse. Throughout the story, Indiana follows these character trajectories through to their natural conclusion, often to dire consequences.

Aside from the twisty story, *Tentacle* is complex and challenging in that it draws influence from sources as disparate as 90's pop culture, contemporary art, queer culture, Dominican *Santeria* and colonial history. There are no parenthetical translations or footnotes to be found anywhere in the book, and some of the points of reference may indeed be new to the average Anglophone reader. This is not a book that holds its readers' hands, and I would not want it to. Rather Indiana and her translator, Achy Obejas, by not patronising her non-Spanish speaking, non-Caribbean readers, are showing a refreshing trust in those readers. In the digital age we live in, it's more than possible to google who Olokun is, to read up on Santeria, Caribbean politics and history – not to mention everything from house music to the work of Goya and his contemporaries. In doing so, we expand our awareness of the world around us a little bit more.

And aside from the real-life themes, the speculative element is glaringly evident in *Tentacle* as well, and the book unapologetically does not fit the "magical realism" box

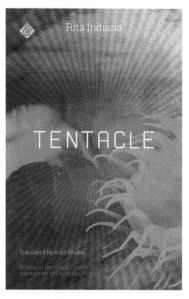

Western readers often seem so keen to place upon any Spanish language fiction. This is science fiction and it doesn't shy away from purely and unequivocally speculative devices – post-apocalyptic narrative, time travel, ecological collapse, cybernetics – and each plays a fundamental role in the narrative. At the same time, though, Indiana seems to have no use for the stock tropes and clichés of contemporary speculative fiction, turning the tired "chosen one" trope on its head. Indiana has used what she needs from the genre and not bothered with the rest.

When it comes down to it, though, *Tentacle* is also fun and exciting, a truly enjoyable read. It's fast-paced, the calm, introspective periods interspersed with peaks of action and sometimes shocking violence. This is an exciting book for the future of the genre, joining the ranks of a new kind of honest, ecological science fiction along the lines of Chen Qiufan. *Tentacle* forces us to question the nature of individual responsibility and culpability, in our personal lives and in the greater narrative of ecological collapse. Indiana's prose and Obejas' translations inject a wry, raw, colourful sensibility into a book that doesn't take itself too seriously. It's well worth reading, as much for fans of old school time travel novels and noir grit as for students of art and contemporary politics. I can't wait for more.

Broken Stars
Edited by Ken Liu
Head of Zeus
464 pages
Review by Calum Barnes

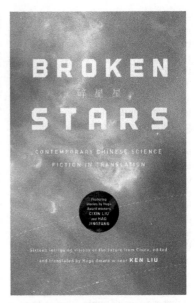

Whilst promoting his latest book, which involves a ménage a trois with an android, Ian McEwan pompously pondered 'there could be an opening of a mental space for novelists to explore this future, not in terms of travelling at 10 times the speed of light in anti-gravity boots, but in actually looking at the human dilemmas of being close up to something that you know to be artificial but which thinks like you." This was of course met with widespread consternation by sci fi writers online who, quite rightly, pointed out that they have been exploring the ethical quandaries thrown up by emergent technologies for years, thank you very much.

Perhaps McEwan would do better to pick up the latest anthology of Chinese science fiction, *Broken Stars*, edited and translated by the indefatigable author translator, Ken Liu. The opening story by Xia Jia, *Goodnight, Melancholy* features Alan Turing and juxtaposes the last years of his life with a speculative future of AI companions in an atomised society, making for a nuanced examination of artificial intelligence and inner life. Unlike McEwan though, this does not have to be quarantined in an alternative past for fear of sullying high literary credentials, the real-life ramifications of AI technologies are richly imagined into the future.

Whilst Liu stresses in his introduction the caveat that this selection only reflects the idiosyncrasies of his own taste, it is nevertheless an expansive range. Fourteen authors, both established and up and coming, spanning hard sci fi thought experiments to lighter pulpier entertainments. He does not, however, kowtow to the comfortable familiarity of Western sci fi tropes and in this anthology features more Chinese specific subgenres.

Zhang Ran's *The Snow of Jinyang* is heavily indebted to 'changyue' , a peculiar form of time travel fiction, infusing historical episodes, in this case tenth century city siege in Northern China, with contemporary technology. Scholars wreak havoc in the realm by ranting on a strange physical internet and 'fire-oil' vehicles trundle around the febrile streets of ancient Jinyang. This delightful mash up of epochs is as much a send up of Imperial China as it is of the bureaucratic machinations of the present. This questioning of historical progress is also at the heart of Baoshu's pleasurable and ingeniously constructed yarn *What Has Passed in Kinder Light Shall Appear* in which the narrator is propelled through the history of twentieth century China backwards.

Appending the anthology are essays by Chinese writers that helpfully contextualise this golden age of science fiction within a distinct literary tradition, as well as a tortured history of state repression throughout the twentieth century. With this new cultural confidence, stories become more self-conscious, evident in the metafictional hue of some of the tales. Fei Dao's *The Robot Who Tells Tall Tales* is a surreal galactic fable worthy of Stanislaw Lem in which a robot travels the universe to collect tales to impress the "Bullshit King" as well as Anna Wu's story set in a restaurant at the end of the universe reflecting on the sacrifices a writer must make to ensure their literary immortality.

The anthology is capped by the two stories of Chen Qiufan. It feels like the coronation of a new king, as it coincides with the publication of Quifan's first novel in English this year, *Waste Tide*, a dystopian thriller set on an e-waste recycling island. Qiufan brings a more leftist cyberpunk sensibility to the scene, a social conscience for a rapidly modernising China. His first story spiritual vacuity of Silicon Valley entrepreneurialism is exposed and his Ballardian anthropology 'A History of Future Illnesses' functions as an exhibition of quiet atrocities yet to come at the hands of both technological and cosmic phenomena. Despite what the stunted middlebrow imaginations of the Ian McEwans of this world may think, Qiufan is already writing from the frontlines of a future that is much closer than most are willing to believe.

Wild Sun
Ehsan Ahmad and Shakil Ahmad
Uproar Books,
326 pages
Review by Suki Hollywood

Wild Sun is set on the planet of Corvos, the humanoid citizens of which live in slavery under the the the Vitaari, a race of interstellar serial colonizers who have recently begun to plunder the planet's natural resources using their superior technology and alien physical strength. The first in a trilogy, this debut novel follows three point of view characters; Cerrin, a 'Katniss Everdeen style' loner who prefers the wilderness of Corvos. Sonus, a mild-mannered former engineer who earns his way into his overseers' good graces, and Captain Vellerik, a Vitaari soldier who wants to make it to retirement with his wife honourably, despite the disruptive arrival of dastardly aristocratic commander, Count Talazeer.

Each narrative thread pulses with intrigue and excitement, the plot pushing forward at rapid and engaging rate, as the three characters confront their own powerlessness. Relying on dramatic and demonstrative acts of cruelty rather than the daily grind of the dehumanisation to provide Cerrin and Sonus with motivation makes for a thrilling read, if at times the extreme violence feels cheapened by the pace. The inclusion of aging Captain Vellerik's perspective allows us insight not only to the world of Corvos, but glimpses into the far reaches of the Vitaari empire, hinting at the massive potential for the two slated sequels.

Another strength of the novel is its refusal to homogenize the indigenous people of Corvos. Cerrin and Sonus' differing origins depict a bustling planet with separate social groups of people who have their conflicts with each other; though Sonus is a former citizen of a rapidly advancing society, Cerrin often reminisces about her tribal childhood, about gods of war and hunting. The lush forests, giant waterlilies and jungle animals of Corvos do suggest it is symbolic of our own natural world, and there is certainly a CliFi element to *Wild Sun*. The Vitaari can be read as a commentary on modern human colonizers and the violence they continue to wreck on both our ecosystems and the indigenous people who live there. They consume food from small boxes, wrapped in clear film, they have white, glittering skin and view their slaves as animalistic. However, the diversity of Corvos' inhabitants create a refreshingly real place with an identity that not solely symbolic, and not reliant only on the narrative of colonisation. At times, these worldbuilding details are sketched – such as the vague belief system

that Cerrin refers to, or the narcotic technology in which Captain Vellerik finds solace – creating more of a playground for action than a world that will appeal to readers pour over the maps at the start of a novel.

The contrasting perspectives of Cerrin, Sonus and Captain Vellerik also allows co-writers Ehsan and Shakil Ahmad to explore not just the heroism of rebellion but the risks of it, as the three characters navigate the dilemma of gravely endangering others while empowering themselves. Overthrowing the Vitaari is important, but the Ahmad's give legitimacy to the desire to simply survive, giving the indigenous slaves interpersonal relationships with each other fraught tension. Though Sonus considers those who rebel to be playing heroes, Cerrin despises those who refuse to fight. On occasion, *Wild Sun* moves away from a recognisable story of good people uniting to overthrow evil, reminiscent of Cameron's *Avatar*, and towards a mediation on the nature of leadership and long terms effects of brutalisation on the brutalised.

This isn't limited to Corvos' indigenous people, as some of the occupying forces are also depicted as victims of the Vitaari elite. Kadessis, a Vitaari historian forced into military service, tells Sonus, "you know, what happens amongst our people is not so different from what happens here... they may wreck the economy, neglect their people, make awful ridiculous mistakes. And yet they remain at the top, looking down upon the rest of us." Marl, a snakelike inhabitant of another colonised planet and violent bodyguard to Count Talazeer, is another example of *Wild Sun*'s refusal to categorise the colonised as heroes and the colonizers as victims. Rebellion is not necessarily heroic, but as gritty and violent as subjugation; a hard pill to swallow, but possibly one that makes for a more interesting read.

Wild Sun is a debut both for its co-writing team, American brothers Ehsan and Shakil Ahmad, and for its publishers, the newly launched Science Fiction and Fantasy focused *Uproar Books*. Both immensely readable and highly ambitious, the finale of *Wild Sun* sets the stage for a page turning trilogy with potential.

The People's Republic of Everything
Nick Mamatas
Tachyon Publications
336 pages
Review by Megan Turney

The People's Republic of Everything is a rather eclectic collection of 15 short stories written by Nick Mamatas, plucked out from various stages of his extensive career as an author, that explore a multitude of genres, perspectives, themes, locations, periods and societal issues. Having already written seven novels, his short stories have also appeared in publications such as *Best American Mystery Stories, Year's Best Science Fiction & Fantasy*, and a list of others that are mentioned throughout his story notes. Many of his short stories have been nominated for awards, in addition to the various other awards and nominations he has received in recognition of his editorial work on numerous anthologies and translated Japanese science-fiction, such as for the Hugo, Locus, World Fantasy, Bram Stoker, Shirley Jackson and International Horror Guild awards.

The People's Republic of Everything is truly an assortment of Mamatas' own distinct style that serves to highlight the vast diversity he explores in his literature. In fact, I would have trouble classifying the collection as whole; instead, it seems more appropriate to describe it as a product and projection of Mamatas' varying interests, opinions and talents that have been developed over the years he's been writing and editing. I would argue that having such an incredibly varied medley of short stories does generally work in his favour; the collection not only provides the reader with quite a vivid image of who Mamatas is as a writer, and from where he derives his wealth of ideas, but it also delivers a collection in which there is bound to be at least one story that appeals to them, whether they're a fan of science-fiction, fantasy, horror, speculative fiction or anything in between.

Yet, admittedly, a disadvantage of this style for me was that, whilst I really enjoyed the stories that aligned with the genres and themes I'm most interested in, I found myself struggling through those that were inspired by subgenres I wouldn't usually pick out for myself; for example, the stories that delve into variants of steampunk, or those that dabble too heavily with form and appearance over content. This was generally exacerbated by, what felt like, a focus on fulfilling the style of a genre rather than developing the characters or general believability; although this can be expected in a short story to a certain extent, it did occasionally result in a lack of depth and context, and the odd struggle here and there in following some of the storylines. Unfortunately, I didn't always enjoy the nature of the narrative style or voice either, which was not so much of a problem during the stories where both the storyline and the characters were so captivating that it didn't really matter, but it was particularly distinct in parts of the collection where Mamatas' 'infamous acid wit' and criticism were quite intense, which resulted in a somewhat uncomfortable read. However, as I do recognise that these are mainly issues of personal taste, I should clarify that I would still recommend the collection as a whole, as those stories that I did enjoy were certainly worth the read.

In fact, when looking back at the collection, it was those jolting, style-driven stories that often provided the necessary juxtaposition to contrast with, and magnify, the more subdued, arguably more powerful, stories where Mamatas' writing skills are at their strongest. These were, for me, those that were grounded in every-day life, in some sort of normalcy, but nonetheless still contained that necessary twist that transforms them into their own surreal amalgamation of science fiction, fantasy and horror. In this way, the collection works well as an overall experience, as the reader is essentially just thrown from one tale into the next, from one unique location, perspective or situation to the next extraordinary self-contained story. Indeed, even with finding issue

with some elements of Mamatas' style and approach, this sense of unpredictability and experimentation did work in heightening the overall eccentric nature of the collection.

The stories that I found most intriguing were those that were, as Mamatas describes them, 'slice-of-life stories'. The stories centred around human relationships, whether that was looking at the interactions between bickering neighbours and a mysterious barking dog, or even just exploring the thought-provoking events set in motion after finding a grandmother's collection of pulp sci-fi magazines. So rather than trying to fit the story into a particular style, the reader is given a chance in these texts to pick out the subtle nods to genres from which Mamatas gets his inspiration and enjoy his writing at its best. For those who also favour literature that delves into the 'human' side of science fiction, fantasy, horror and speculative fiction, I would strongly recommend the short stories: 'A Howling Dog'; 'The Spook School'; 'The People's Republic of Everywhere and Everything'; 'The Phylactery'; 'Dreamer of the Day'; and, my personal favourite, 'Tom Silex, Spirit-Smasher'.

Blood Bath Literary Zine – The Bodies Issue
Edited by Katy Lennon
61 Pages
Review by Callum McSorley

From the wonderful black-and-white cover art by Jo Ruessman, you know you are in for something special as soon as you pick up a copy of Blood Bath Literary Magazine's inaugural issue. Called *The Bodies Issue*, it features thirteen short stories and poems on the theme of 'bodies', edited by Katy Lennon.

The opening story by Ever Dundas,

'Miss West's Requisitions', lives up to the name of the magazine, delivering the kind of gore of which Tom Savini would be proud . The image of irritating colleague Ken's body dismantled and wired up to become a scanner and printer (scanning with gouged eyeballs, printing with blood, of course) is one you'll find hard to shake, although as part of a tale of nine-to-five, office-work drudgery, it's as comical as it is gruesome.

Another stand-out short story in the collection is Scott Clark's 'Family Pool'. A Cronenbergian body-horror piece, it's about a troubled family's new swimming pool which appears to be infested with something that loves eating steak and is causing them to swap body parts and melt together. The way the narrator's voice shifts and changes until you are no longer sure whose point of view you're experiencing is a clever touch, and its epistolary form (usually the reserve of gothic) works well.

'Feed Them' by Mary Crosbie is also about water monsters, though in this case they're internal. Protagonist Vera has agreed to an experimental weight-loss programme which finds her wanting to eat people. Crosbie's tale captures one of the central themes of The Bodies Issue: shame. The feeling of shame about the way your body looks and smells and its natural functions is the core feature of many of the stories here. Vera was ashamed of being overweight and made miserable by her embarrassed mother, causing her to take drastic action.

Elizabeth Guttery, in Rita Hynes's 'The Unrecalled', is similarly shunned for her body odour, but unlike Vera, she defies those who would make her ashamed. She refuses to wash and is fascinated by the natural smells and functions of her body, and is almost morbidly interested in her periods, convinced she is "dying all the time".

Blood Bath
Literary Zine

The
BODIES
Issue

Hynes directly tackles mainstream culture's traditional squeamishness around female bodies, which seeks to hide and cover-up and control them.

Unfortunately, what we learn in Hynes's tale is that outsiders must change or die, which brings us to the other big theme of The Bodies Issue: transformation.

A character turns to stone in 'Petrified' by Felicity Anderson-Nathan, a werewolf narrates Laura DeHaan's poem 'Enclosed in Clothes', Vera is drastically losing weight, and Scott Clark's pool-dwelling family is merging together and becoming each other. Both horror and triumph come from transformation. It can be both terrifying and freeing.

We also have transformation of old stories into new, with retellings of Sleeping Beauty and The Little Mermaid by Alys Earl and Angie Spoto, respectively. In Earl's 'The Eye That Offends You', the princesses's beauty is so great it is unbearable to look at and drives people mad – beauty itself becomes something terrible. However, if there is a small criticism to be made, it's that these particular pieces don't offer the kind of fresh subversion of the horror genre found in the other stories and poems. Recent times have seen fairytale revisions in the style of Angela Carter having become a popular horror subgenre in their own right.

That said, the magazine as a whole is not only brimming with gruesome menace, it has a relevant place in the vibrant Scottish indie publishing scene. In her introduction, Lennon writes of the stories she has collected: "None of them can be read without leaving you with a dark comment on an aspect of modern society." And this is true. Whether it's about fat-shaming, period-shaming, or fear of the Other – something that has forever been inextricably linked to people's bodies inside and out– these stories have something to say beyond just grossing you out or giving you the creeps (though they do that just fine too!)

The magazine is a political statement in its itself. As Lennon says, Blood Bath Literary Zine is "Confirmation… that the type of horror I wanted to see on the literary scene could exist. It could be weird, emotional, it could subvert genre and literary conventions, it could be lyrical and politically aware, and did not have to be wholly dominated by cis white men." This is the joy, and importance, of independent publishing. Small publishers can implement the changes they want to see in the larger industry with ease. Blood Bath is not dominated by cis white men, it's diverse and inclusive and for the next issue (on the theme of 'demons') it is focus is diversity of publishing, including a focus on people colour.

Horror, as a genre, shook off its reputation as juvenile and trashy some time ago, and this generation's rediscovery of its greats, like Shirley Jackson, has pushed it into the mainstream to serious, critical appraisal. But horror will always be at home with independent creators, the B-movie makers and the zine-staplers, where you find things at their most weird, their most unique, their most terrifying.

***Blood Bath 2: Demons* is out now from www.bloodbathlitzine.com**

This is not the sort of rescue Hollywood has trained him for

They do not watch the news that morning, but
They go to the beach and have ice-cream
for breakfast.

                everybody knows.

            And the beach is full
            of people having ice-cream for breakfast
                 in the shadow of the rockets.

He brings the giant chalks and they join
the ones who are cave-painting
on the walls of the city. Switch to felt pens
to make stained glass of the buildings

                 their short lives

And it is all tremendous fun.

        we thought were the future.

And they do not watch the news that lunchtime.
They go home and get in the car
and he sits them in turn on his knee

               and they drive
               while he does the pedals.

They bake and build Lego and play all the games
and they both cheat
They eat

               and he lets them cheat.
        when they want
               and they eat what they want
               and the rockets are boarding

and when it gets dark they run outside
in their socks and stay up to watch the bats
and star-spot in the clutter of the night sky

        because it's important
               to keep your promises.

They shh and beam and giggle.

        It is way past bedtime.

And they do not watch the news that evening,
but he knows all the same
it is time to sleep,

        the first bomb has dropped,
               the rockets are leaving,
        and it is time to sleep.

So he brings them hot chocolate,
tucks them up with kisses and lies
waiting.

               Their bedtime drink
               makes them so dozy.

Their breathing settles.

        He hugs the spare pillow to his chest

Angela Cleland

The Holodeck

The floor moves with me as I walk. I can never outrun it. I conceived this earth-walk as a grand escape. Planned my route as if winding yarn about the world. Won't miss an inch. It started well, with forests of synthetic green, deer leaping invisible hurdles, more – cities, deserts, ice. And now my daughter joins me. But by now I am walking the ocean floor, have been for weeks. We walk in silence. See nothing but a slow-moving spider-crab, the picked-clean bone hull of a whale. *Is this what it's like?* she asks. *Earth, is this why you left?* She tries to catch my eye. *Mostly,* I say and take her hand. The floor moves with us as we walk.

Angela Cleland

Angela Cleland was born in Scotland and now lives in Surrey. She has published two poetry collections, *And in Here the Menagerie* (Templar Poetry, 2007) and *Room of Thieves* (Salt, 2013), and one science fiction novel, *Sequela*. She is currently working on a fantasy novel and a third poetry collection.
Twitter: @AngelaCleland

Seeding the Coalsack

There are no stars;
the sky's dark depths
are ornamented only by
three moons which gleam
with light from our old
dully crimson sun
that fails to warm
the planet's
daytime face.

Space ripples... once... again...
and as a third distortion
rips across the violet sky,
it's there: a sudden bubble,
iridescent steel, a spurt of flame
so bright
we're blinded for a while,
as if in punishment
for catching sight of gods.

Gods they were not, though —
no, nothing like; they brought
disturbance, discontent,
division where we'd been at one.
Fear we'd have coped with,
welcomed even, seeing it as due to real
divinities. Instead they made us
long for distances,   want what we
desire the stars.   had not conceived.

We had no choice;   Regret is futile;
what our former gods had once demanded
we now did,   and not in mockery;
these shining visitors died hard,
uncomprehending,
but we did them honour
as we sacramentally
prepared their
alien,
unappetising
carcases.

Peter King

125

Setting Out

We find a path here, wriggling our steps
round features such as clumps of fern,
bare outcrops of a crumbling grey rock,
small pools of brackish water clogged with weed.
Sometimes it detours past a patch
of level, clear, and ordinary ground —
whoever made it maybe had a different
notion of what constitutes an obstacle.

We hear sounds: a few suggest intention
(songs or twitterings; the grunts of
unknown creatures rooting in the undergrowth),
most not (the creak of branches in the wind,
the varied tunes of water falling, flowing,
finding its own level).
We scent sweet blossom, pungent herbs,
decaying vegetation,
and the reek of days-dead corpses.

If we're not clear as to our destination,
then neither is the path we tread; the landscape
changes, varying with soil, with climate,
altitude, and habitation.

We come upon a city, giant buildings
housing creatures in proportion,
gazes fixed above our heads;
their conversations hint at things that
seem familiar, but are just beyond our grasp.
Yet here we feel a certain safety, wandering
among them, making strangeness less alarming.
Still we pass them by, but carry with us
something of a sense of purpose,
though we cannot pin it down.
And sooner than we had expected,
our remembrance dims; what was it like,
to walk among those people?
Some of us, perhaps, have clearer recollections,
but cannot pass them on.

We press ahead. We think the path is little changed,
but can't compare — we try, but can't look back.

Peter King

Utopian

This used to be all tower blocks and office building.
It used to house people like trapped mice.

These fields held roads and tin cans for roaming types,
these willowed gardens were warehoused shelves of ripe food

and occasional hedge trimmers cutting rose cankers in a sea
of money trees. People, like the ants that own it now,

hollowed into their spaces and hid,
watching and tapping and watching and tapping,

unboxing parcels inside their brick boxes
scattering the remains across the earth

and mountains of oil in bright coloured pieces
that crawled from the ocean, into the air

swallowed them up, their carping
goldfish mouths, gaping and gasping.

Rachel Sambrooks

Peter J. King's poetry and prose, including translations from German and
modern Greek, has been published in numerous journals.
His latest collections are *Adding Colours to the Chameleon* (2016, Wisdom's
Bottom Press) and *All What Larkin* (2017, Albion Beatnik Press – second,
expanded edition due out this year).

Fallopian Holiday

I know, I know, I shouldn't have it fitted.
I was out on the prowl, desperately seeking baby land.
Nanobot fixed not-preggo situation, fixed the twist, refused to leave.
A nano holidaying in my fallopian tube.

Message sent: warm and nice
Message sent: egg released
Message sent: load downloaded
Message sent: Mummy

Rachel Sambrooks

Rachel Sambrooks has published two collections *Stand By Your Nan* funded by
Arts Council England on tour 2018 and *The Strangest Sandwich in the World*
longlisted for the CLiPPA award. She runs Words Aloud, a friendly spoken word
event at Sutton Library where she is Writer in Residence for 2019.

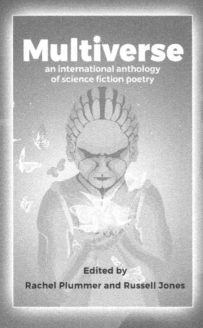

CONER '17

BECOME A PATRON

SHORELINE OF INFINITY HAS A *PATREON* PAGE AT

WWW.PATREON.COM/ SHORELINEOFINFINITY

ON *PATREON*, YOU CAN PLEDGE A MONTHLY PAYMENT FROM *AS LOW AS $1* IN EXCHANGE FOR A *COOL TITLE* AND A *REGULAR REWARD.*

ALL PATRONS GET AN *EARLY DIGITAL ISSUE* OF THE MAGAZINE QUARTERLY AND *EXCLUSIVE ACCESS* TO OUR PATREON MESSAGE FEED AND SOME GET *A LOT MORE.* HOW ABOUT THESE?

POTENT PROTECTOR SPONSORS A STORY EVERY YEAR WITH FULL CREDIT IN THE MAGAZINE WHILE AN *AWESOME AEGIS* SPONSORS AN ILLUSTRATION.

TRUE BELIEVER SPONSORS A *BEACHCOMBER COMIC* AND *MIGHTY MENTOR* SPONSORS A COVER PICTURE.

AND .... OUR HIGHEST HONOUR ... *SUPREME SENTINEL* SPONSORS A *WHOLE ISSUE* OF SHORELINE OF INFINITY.

ASK *YOUR FAVOURITE BOOK SHOP* TO GET YOU A COPY. WE ARE ON THE *TRADE DISTRIBUTION LISTS.*

OR BUY A COPY *DIRECTLY* FROM OUR *ONLINE SHOP* AT

WWW.SHORELINEOFINFINITY.COM

YOU CAN GET AN *ANNUAL SUBSCRIPTION* THERE TOO.

KINDLE FANS CAN GET SHORELINE FROM THE *AMAZON KINDLE STORE*

Lightning Source UK Ltd.
Milton Keynes UK
UKHW022017180619
344604UK00005B/308/P